D1246424

Dear Readers:

Mother always said she wanted her books to be good enough to be found in someone's attic!

After all of these years, I find her stories—not in attics at all—but prominent in fans' bookcases just as mine are. It is so heart-warming to know that through these republications she will go on telling good stories and being there for her "girls," some of whom find no other place to turn.

With a heart full of love and pride–
Janet Lambert's daughter,
Jeanne Ann Vanderhoef

Little Miss Atlas

✳✳✳

Books by Janet Lambert

PENNY PARRISH STORIES
Star Spangled Summer 1941
Dreams of Glory 1942
Glory Be! 1943
Up Goes the Curtain 1946
Practically Perfect 1947
The Reluctant Heart 1950

TIPPY PARRISH STORIES
Miss Tippy 1948
Little Miss Atlas 1949
Miss America 1951
Don't Cry Little Girl 1952
Rainbow After Rain 1953
Welcome Home, Mrs. Jordan 1953
Song in Their Hearts 1956
Here's Marny 1969

JORDAN STORIES
Just Jenifer 1945
Friday's Child 1947
Confusion by Cupid 1950
A Dream for Susan 1954
Love Taps Gently 1955
Myself & I 1957
The Stars Hang High 1960
Wedding Bells 1961
A Bright Tomorrow 1965

PARRI MACDONALD STORIES
Introducing Parri 1962
That's My Girl 1964
Stagestruck Parri 1966
My Davy 1968

CANDY KANE STORIES
Candy Kane 1943
Whoa, Matilda 1944
One for the Money 1946

DRIA MEREDITH STORIES
Star Dream 1951
Summer for Seven 1952
High Hurdles 1955

CAMPBELL STORIES
The Precious Days 1957
For Each Other 1959
Forever and Ever 1961
Five's a Crowd 1963
First of All 1966
The Odd Ones 1969

SUGAR BRADLEY STORIES
Sweet as Sugar 1967
Hi, Neighbor 1968

CHRISTIE DRAYTON STORIES
Where the Heart Is 1948
Treasure Trouble 1949

PATTY AND GINGER STORIES
We're Going Steady 1958
Boy Wanted 1959
Spring Fever 1960
Summer Madness 1962
Extra Special 1963
On Her Own 1964

CINDA HOLLISTER STORIES
Cinda 1954
Fly Away Cinda 1956
Big Deal 1958
Triple Trouble 1965
Love to Spare 1967

LITTLE
MISS ATLAS

By
JANET LAMBERT

Image Cascade Publishing

www.ImageCascade.com

MANUFACTURED IN THE UNITED STATES
OF AMERICA

A hardcover edition of this book was originally published
by E. P. Dutton & Co. It is here reprinted by arrangement
with Mrs. Jeanne Ann Vanderhoef.

First *Image Cascade Publishing* edition published 2000.

Library of Congress Cataloging in Publication Data
Lambert, Janet 1895-1973
        Little miss atlas.

(Juvenile Girls)
Reprint. Originally published: New York: E. P.
Dutton, 1949.

ISBN 978-1-930009-19-6

Dear Girls:

I can't tell you how very happy your letters make me. I love to read them, to know the things you do, the things you think, and that you enjoy my books. I open each one eagerly but, and this makes me so terribly sad—I can't answer them. Perhaps it seems that I could, but I'm sure you'll understand why it is impossible for me to manage it when I explain it to you.

Each letter is just one letter from you, one very treasured letter which I keep and sometimes re-read, but it's one of hundreds of letters each year, to me. Today, I had six. And if I were to answer those six letters, I couldn't write my chapter of "Little Miss Atlas" which must be finished tonight before I put my typewriter away. If I were to answer *all* the letters, I couldn't write two books a year for you. And if I didn't write you the books, you wouldn't write me the letters. So, you see, we have a circle. You give me your letters and I give you my books. And your letters are an inspiration to me, for they tell me what stories you like the best, what characters, and what families.

I hope you won't stop sending me the letters; because you know, now, why I can't answer them and that they mean a great deal to me. I love them.

You ask me so many questions in your letters, the main one being: will I write more books? Girls, I'll write books forever if you want to read them. I like doing it, and as long as my four typing fingers hold out I'll think up plots. There

[5]

will be another book about Tippy, probably next Fall; Alcie Jordon, in the Spring; Christy Drayton will squeeze in, too; and perhaps we'll find a new family every once in awhile. I'm as curious about these people as you are, and since I want to know what happens to them all, we'll follow them together and find out. After all, they're more important to you than I am.

So please accept this letter, each one of you, as your own personal correspondence from me and forgive me for not sending it in an envelope, with an address and a stamp.

Lovingly and gratefully,

P.S. Those of you who care to, might even write and tell me you understand. Oh, I do hope you will!

[6]

Little Miss Atlas

✻✻✻

CHAPTER I

THE ship rolled, or perhaps merely curtsied a farewell to New York harbor, and sent Mrs. Parrish backward against a small metal locker. "Oh, my goodness," she said, taking off her hat that the closet's swinging door had knocked over her eyes, "I haven't my sea legs, yet."

She surveyed the tiny stateroom. The best army transport is not a luxury liner, and this one was not one of the best. Along each side wall ran a set of triple-decker beds reaching almost to the ceiling, and each bed was heaped with suitcases, coats, boxes and the impedimenta necessary to travel. The narrow center aisle was completely filled by her daughter, who, with a foot on one bottom bed, was stretched across to a top one on the opposite side, trying to reach a toilet case. There was no place for Mrs. Parrish to lay her hat, so after holding it indecisively for a moment, she set it back on her head. "Tippy," she asked mildly, "do you think you could straighten up for a second so I could play 'London Bridge' and get past you?"

"Could do." Tippy Parrish pressed her hands against the bed, curved herself in an arch, and waited for her mother's mashed hat to go under. "I'm hot," she complained, when the path was clear again. "How about calling off the settling in until I can peel off this jacket?"

"It's all right with me, but where are you planning to put it?"

"How about hanging it in the locker?" She jumped down and fished a bedraggled handkerchief from her pocket. The handkerchief was still damp from tears she had shed into it before squaring her shoulders for the march up the gang-plank, and it felt cool against her forehead. She rubbed back her short curls that salt air and perspiration had turned into a halo of ringlets and turned sad hazel eyes on the open locker. "Full," she commented briefly. "Two hangers worth, and it's full."

Tippy had dimples at the corner of her mouth that often acted as blinker lights, winking on and off and giving her an elfin charm. They flashed briefly as she surveyed the locker, then her lips met in a grim line and she sat down on the bottom bed. "This," she remarked, peeking out at her mother, "is, as Bobby would say, 'the end of the limit.'"

"I suppose so, but where can we put our clothes?"

"Just spread 'em out on the top four beds, I guess; we can only sleep in two."

Tippy had lost interest in the clothes. She wriggled out of her brown suit jacket and let it drop behind her, unbuttoned the white cuffs of her silk blouse, loosened its lacy collar, and sat with her eyes on her new suede pumps that hurt. She felt much too dressed up for a warm September day when she should have been at home in shorts, dashing around in her own familiar world on Governors Island; planning for school to open; to swim; to see a movie with her gang; and she announced, unhappily, "The army defeats me. I don't want to live in Germany, and I wish Dad had retired when he got wounded."

Her mother sighed with her, but she had found a place for her hat by clapping it on a light fixture beside the wash basin. "Don't be silly. We all love the army," she reproved gently, just as she always had when things seemed impossible, but at the same time wondering where she could put the *bon voyage* basket of fruit that sat on the floor at her feet.

"Quit staring at that basket," Tippy said glumly, reading her thoughts. "I'll sleep with it for a pillow. I told you it **was** foolish to bring it along."

"But Penny's cook gave it to us," her mother protested. "She went all the way in to New York and . . ."

"I know, you told me. 'Minna carried it all the way home on the train and Penny was *so* pleased, *so* proud.' "

Tippy wanted to topple over on the clean white spread and bury her face in the neat square of olive drab army blanket that was folded on the foot of her bed. Right at this very minute Penny was cool and comfortable, driving along the broad country highway with her husband, toward her own beautiful house and her baby. Penny's darned lucky, she thought, to have been old enough to get married and miss all this. Of course, she feels sad about Mums and me going away, but it will wear off in two shakes because she has Josh and little Parri. We're the ones who have to keep on suffering. And Bobby, the big stupe, gets to stay home and go to college. At that, she poked her head out and demanded, "Why, do you suppose, Bobby would ever choose the army for a career? Why would he *ever* be dumb enough to want to go to West Point?"

"Because he's a soldier's son," her mother answered, disposing of her basket by crowding it under the loop of nickel pipe that made the wash basin efficient.

"And so's David, but he got out. He resigned."

"He's a farmer's great-grandson," her mother reminded absently, while she wondered how much more the basin could accommodate, counting from the light down and with coat hangers hooked here and there. "And Carrol had a big estate that had to be managed. When you have a lovely wife like Carrol, and a little son. . . ." She stopped and made a brisk effort of moving her coat from one bed to another, but Tippy crawled out of her cavern and put both arms around her.

"Mums," she said, "it's no good. We're both terribly homesick for our family, and we'll feel lots, lots better if we talk it out. It doesn't help to go around pretending you're glad and gay and off on a lark when you hurt inside. I'm

[11]

homesick, I'll admit it. I'm darned homesick. I even want to see Bobby, and most of the time I'm mad at him."

"All right, darling." Mrs. Parrish released herself and said, while she put the coat back where it had been before, "Perhaps you're right. Where do you think they all are, now?"

"Well, David and Carrol are driving just as fast as they can to the hospital to see little Davy. They love us a lot, but they have to know that Davy is better. And they're talking about Warm Springs and how soon they can take him down there, and wondering, just as they have every day since he got polio, how soon he can walk and should they take baby Lang with them or leave him with Penny like they decided to do. Sometimes they'll stop talking of their own affairs and one or the other will say, 'How far do you suppose Mums and Tip are by now?', but most of the time they'll be thinking about their children."

"And that's exactly as it should be," Mrs. Parrish answered, leaning against the iron upright that held the beds across from Tippy. "I shouldn't ever want it to be any different."

"No, but I'll bet Penny's crying all over Josh. I'll bet he's having a time." Tippy let her dimples flash out because talking eased the aching hurt inside her chest. It had the same effect as an aspirin, and while the pain would come back, many times during her stay in Europe, it would never be quite so acute or tormenting as now. So she said, "Penny can bear up better than anybody in the family—except you," she added gallantly and with great honesty. "But she can break up in more pieces afterward and cry harder, too."

"Perhaps that's why she's such a successful actress, or perhaps she's reached her success because of it," her mother answered.

"Do you think she'll go on with it, the acting, I mean, now that she's turned down the new play and a movie?"

"I don't know, honey. Penny is so afraid that something might happen to little Parri as it did to Davy, and so eager for a new baby that she may never act again. She's such a dear, sweet child. No one in the whole world is more loving than Penny, or. . . ." Mrs. Parrish broke off and fussed with the coat again, and Tippy said quickly:

"I guess I'm making it harder for you, Mums. I'm being selfish, I guess."

"No, you aren't, darling. I love them all so much, David and Bobby and Penny. And Carrol and Josh are like my own, too, and the three little ones. I'm never away from them, dear. That's what you must learn. No matter where you are, you are *never* away from the ones you love."

"I'll bet Trudy told you that." Tippy looked up from her perch on the bed and added, "It sounds just like her."

"Yes, she said it." The memory of Trudy's dear brown face held them both. Trudy's hands folded over her starched white apron, her never-failing words of love and wisdom.

"Oh, I hope she'll be happy at Penny's," Tippy whispered. "Trudy's not just our cook, she's part of us; and I've never, in all my life, been so far away from her before."

"She will be. And it won't be for long. Two years will pass and. . . ."

"Two years! Oh, dear." She shook her head dismally from side to side, and her mother felt it was time to leave America and turn their thoughts to the continent that lay ahead.

"Look, honey," she suggested, "if we don't want Dad to meet us ten days from now and find two wailing women sitting in a mess, we had better—and I quote him, 'hump our stumps.' "

"Thanks for calling me a woman." Tippy crawled out of her cave again and, since there was no room for her at the end of the room by the wash basin, struck a pose before the locker and the outside door. "You throw me everything that belongs up here," she said, "and I'll pitch you what I can't get in. What we can't stow away we'll shove out the porthole."

"That might solve the problem."

Mrs. Parrish went over to measure the space between a bed and the floor, and was pushing a box into it when there was a knock on the door. "Oh, me!" she cried. "What do you suppose I've left undone that I should have taken care of? I have all the papers David told me to keep and the card for our table in the dining room at the second sitting. I get my passport back tomorrow and the man said not to worry about it, and fifty copies of Dad's travel orders and ours are in that silly brief case. You answer, Tip. I can't get past you."

So Tippy closed the locker, held the knob to keep it shut, and opened the door.

A young red-haired officer stood in the corridor and he asked, "Miss Parrish?"

"Yes."

"Is your mother here?"

Tippy tried to control a giggle as she swung the door wider open and displayed her mother against the opposite wall. Mrs. Parrish's hat, from its perch on the light bulb, seemed to sit on top of her head; and she held an umbrella she had been using to poke the box under the bed. "There she is," Tippy answered just as her mother, with rather a strange effect, stepped out from under her hat.

The young officer smiled, too, and he let his grin widen when she laughed with him. But he sobered enough to say, "I'm Captain Brereton, and I think I bring you good news."

"Oh, dear me, come in if you can." She gestured with informal hospitality while Tippy backed down the aisle. But he only stepped inside the door and said quickly:

"Colonel Mears, the transport commander, asked me to come and tell you that we had a cancellation at the last minute. General and Mrs. Collem didn't sail with us and he would like to offer you their stateroom. I can tell you it's much more comfortable than this one," he added into her stunned surprise. "It's up forward in the section reserved for ranking officers who travel with their wives—and it has a bath."

"Oh, happy day!" Tippy had seen the better part of the ship where *Off limit* signs were posted, and she dived for her coat while her mother wasted precious time in polite amenities. "Let's move," she urged, preparing to carry all the luggage herself and as much as possible in one load.

But Captain Brereton turned his grin on. "Let the steward bring it," he said to her. "They'll put everything in and all you have to do is come with me."

"Gladly!" Tippy reached him in one long stride and not caring that her mother was reminding her about the box concealed under the bed and was searching for her purse and brief case. The brief case was to become as much a part of them during their long journey to Europe and across the occupied country of Germany as the clothes they wore. It was to accompany them on every trip they might take in the future, filled with passports, travel orders, maps and lists of instructions; but for one day at least, it had fulfilled its duty and was locked and put away, and Tippy had seen enough of it. It was important to Mrs. Marjorie Landers Parrish, wife of David G. Parrish, Colonel of Cavalry, and to Miss Andrea Lee Parrish, daughter. But no one else could travel on the printed words it contained, so she said, "Oh, leave it here, Mums, it's safe," and rushed out into the corridor.

Captain Brereton held the door for her mother, and Mrs. Parrish smiled as she passed him, her brief case safely tucked under her arm. "We have to keep track of our papers, don't we?" she asked, lifting her eyebrows, and looking up earnestly.

"We sure do." Her brown eyes were sweetly serious and her soft brown hair had gray wings at the temples. He knew

[15]

she was trying to be competent; and, having seen the Parrish clan gathered around her on the deck before sailing, knew, too, that she was a little sad and unsure of her future. So he took the brief case and said companionably, "The army has a lot of red tape connected with traveling. But when you think that this one ship, alone, holds as many people as a small village, and that at least one or two transports sail every week, it's amazing how the thing can be done at all. Thousands of us are pouring into Germany, complete with families."

"Have you a wife?" she turned to ask, and starting Tippy along the corridor.

"A wife and two children," he answered. "Little ones, that will be a tough job for Mary for the next ten days. All of us young officers have to work just as hard as if we were on an army post. Officer of the day, guard duty, and. . . ." He stopped to explain, "We have thirteen hundred troops aboard. I've got ninety-two quartered in one big dormitory."

They had come to an intersection at the end of the corridor and he motioned Tippy to turn left. "Your cabin's on the port side," he said, motioning another turn but to the right this time. "It will be cooler when we get in the Gulf Stream—at least so they tell me, I don't know why. Here it is."

The door to a room stood open and they stopped and looked inside. It was twice the size of the one they had left, and only one double-decker bed was against the wall.

"My soul," Tippy said, stepping inside. "I wish you'd look. It has a desk with drawers underneath, and two lockers, and two real chairs. *And a bathroom!* A cute little tiled *bathroom!*"

"Oh, it's lovely." Mrs. Parrish looked about the room, too, then turned to the young man beside her. "I can't ever thank you enough," she said. "I feel awfully selfish but we're surely happy to have it."

"It's Colonel Mears you have to thank," he told her. "Although your moving up here will ease things for a sergeant's

[16]

wife who has three children and only two beds to put them in. They tried to bolt in an extra crib for her but it was the last one left and was broken. She'll think she's in Heaven when she moves into the room you've left."

"Then I feel better about it." Mrs. Parrish took her brief case and laid it on top of the built-in desk and held out her hand. "Please thank Colonel Mears for me," she said, "until I meet him and thank him, myself."

"I will. And your stuff will be right over. Just relax and enjoy the trip."

When the door had closed behind him, Tippy flopped into the straight arm chair that had a padded seat and stretched out her legs. "Do you know what I'm going to do?" she asked, and without waiting for an answer, "I'm going to send a cable to David."

"For mercy's sake, why?"

"Because they were all so worried about that room we had. You could just see it sticking out of their eyes. And they kept looking at each other and hunching up their shoulders as if to say, 'What under the sun can we do about it?' It will be a great relief to them to know we're comfortable."

"But what if you can't send cables on a transport? Perhaps you can't, unless it's for something important, like life or death."

"Well, this is important, and I'll ask Colonel Mears. If he wanted us to be comfortable he'll want our family to know we are. I'll hunt him up and ask him."

"Wait until tonight, dear. He's a very busy man right now; and our family can wait a bit."

"Okay, I'll wait till then." Tippy got up from her chair and prepared to remove her coat again. "We have to unpack, anyway," she said. "We have a good spot over there beyond the desk for the hand trunks, and we each have a locker; and I don't think we'll need to keep out a lot of clothes. It doesn't look as if it will be a very dressy trip, does it?"

[17]

"No, you'll probably want only a couple of print dresses and your slacks for morning, and some shirts and a sweater or two. If you want more it won't be hard to find it."

There was a great deal of bumping and thumping in cabin B-7, but gradually order came out of chaos and Mrs. Parrish sat down to consult a card. "The second sitting for supper is at six o'clock," she said, reading. "That's ours. Breakfast is at eight, lunch at twelve. Do you want to go on deck before supper call?"

"Will you come, too?"

"No, but you run on. I still have a few things here to do."

"You won't be lonesome?" Tippy stood near the door and looked at her mother anxiously. "You won't sigh like you do sometimes, or stare off into space, or—or anything?"

"Of course not, darling."

"You've been doing it."

"I know, but that was when I first started out and hadn't got my second wind." Mrs. Parrish crossed the room and took Tippy's worried face between her two hands. "Listen, sweet," she said, "I'm on my way to meet Dad. At first, I was homesick for my children, which is natural, but now, I'm thinking about seeing Dad. He's my husband, and I love him."

"And you're happy about living in Germany?"

"Of course, honey."

"Well," Tippy gave one of the sighs she had accused her mother of emitting, and grumbled, "I wish *I* had something to get thrilled over."

"You will, Tip, really you will."

"Uh." Tippy opened the door then closed it behind her. She walked slowly along the corridor, saw a door leading to the deck and stepped through it.

The sea looked blue and calm. Far off to her left was a hazy point of land and she studied it. "Might be Fort Hancock," she decided, then shook her head. "No, that's on the other side. Maybe it's Barnegat Light. No, that's somewhere else. Oh, what's the difference? It's the end of these good United States, isn't it? It's the end of all your fun, Tippy Parrish. You go off to Europe at sixteen, right in the best year of your life, and you'll come back an old woman; darned near old enough to vote. And why?" she asked the water, going over to lean on the rail. But the waves flowing past her had only one aim. The prow of the ship had cut them in two with a fine white spray and they raced outward, their crests braced like white sails in the wind, trying to meet and fuse again. So she told them anyway, "You do it because you have to be a policeman to a country that started a war. At least your father does, and you have to go where your father goes. And maybe the people don't want you. I wouldn't. If I got beaten in a war, I'd rather muddle along and lick my wounds privately. I wouldn't want to be rehabilitated. I wouldn't *like* people to come and stare at me; and I'll bet the Germans won't like us. They won't have time or else won't bother to talk to me, and I can't speak their darned old language, anyhow. So I'll just sit. And sit, and sit—with nothing to do. Alice Jordon can stay on Governors Island with the crowd, and can go up to West Point to dances with Peter, even if he is her brother. But not me—not the one he especially invited."

She thought of looking at a photograph of Peter, the one he had given her two hours ago when they had stood close together beside another stretch of rail, but it was in her purse and she could only remember how tall and blond and lean he looked, with his short hair crisply parted, and the brass buttons on his cadet dress uniform marching in a double row from his tight collar down his chest.

Tippy had no real need for the photograph, neither for one of Peter or of Alice under a straight brown bang. Their dear faces were constantly with her, and would be meager and silent company for two long years.

It had seemed still on the deck with only the wash of waves,

[19]

but now she was conscious of noise and clatter and shifted her gloomy thoughts to it. Children's voices came through open portholes, mingled with tired scolding from mothers. A steady racket went on below her that sounded as if someone were trying to rip the ship apart or were rolling an endless chain of garbage cans down an iron stairway. Tippy frowned and listened; and when a snub-nosed boy came by, she turned and asked him, "What's going on, down there?"

"Soldiers' chow line. Gee, it's sumpin." He was a year or so younger than she and more inquisitive. "I saw it," he volunteered. "My dad's a mess sergeant and he took me down. The G.I.'s get their trays and go past a counter for their food. After they finish eating, they stack their dishes on a big table and slam their trays on a pile."

"What are the trays made of, cast iron?"

"Tin." The boy missed the sarcasm in her voice and told her proudly, "My dad said they can put through fifteen hundred men in two hours and feed 'em good. You ought to see the kitchens and the stuff they have to eat. Want to go down, sometime?"

"No, thank you." Food, neither soldiers' nor her own, interested her. She wanted to turn back to the sea and her moodiness, but a voice, tinny from having traveled on a wire, announced above her:

"Second sitting. Second sitting. All persons eating at the second sitting will please come quickly to the dining salon and find your table numbers. There will be no smoking in the dining salon and half an hour will be allowed for each meal. Please do not overstay your time as a third sitting must be prepared for. The dining salon is located on 'C' deck, aft of the lounge. The center stairway will bring you to 'C' deck."

The message was being repeated, but she had heard enough from it and her mother to know she was due somewhere, not for pleasure, but for the business of keeping up her strength. It looked to her as if the whole ship were designed for efficiency and good health, from the sanitary, uncarpeted state-rooms to the corps of doctors and nurses, the hospital, the dispensary, and a special diet kitchen for babies. The Army Transport Service was moving the army and it dared anyone to get sick and throw it out of kilter. So she smiled and said good-by to the boy and started off in the direction he pointed.

"I've eaten. It's good chow," he offered as consolation, and taking an apple from his pocket.

"Thanks, I hope so."

Tippy retraced her steps, found her own door and collected her mother. The stateroom looked neat and almost cozy. The *bon voyage* basket sat on the desk and was flanked by photographs of all the Parrishes; a red-and-white striped knitting bag hung on the arm of a chair, and even the folded army blankets looked less harsh and scratchy.

"Gosh," Tippy said, taking her mother's arm as they walked along the corridor together, "you can sure work wonders."

And the dining room was peacefully quiet, once they had found the stairs again and crossed a small lounge that was filled with running children, screaming babies and hot, tired parents, half-eaten fruit and strewn paper cups. Its round tables were covered with white cloths, and waiters were standing beside them.

"Lovely," Mrs. Parrish said, pleased and looking around eagerly for their table. "Aren't those the Caldwells over there? Why, bless my soul, there's Colonel Wilkins! And they're at number two, and that's our number. Oh, how nice!"

She was busily shaking hands, saying, "You remember Tippy, my youngest, don't you?" and Tippy found herself smiling at Mrs. Caldwell who was fat, at Colonel Caldwell who was thin, and their daughter, Arline, who wore glasses and looked as glum as Tippy felt, and at ruddy Colonel Wilkins who had a shock of gray hair and a bristling black mustache. "How nice," Mrs. Parrish kept repeating as she slid into her chair. "I wonder if there are any more army families on board whom we know? I think it's going to be a lovely crossing."

At that, everyone looked the diners over. They talked and twisted around to see, and while her mother and Mrs. Caldwell covered the years from 1938, Tippy stole time for a private search of her own.

She had just remembered a gay and personable young officer who was supposed to have sailed on this boat. At least Penny had thought he had, and she wished she could ask Colonel Wilkins about him. It should have been easy to halt her soup spoon halfway to her mouth and say casually above it, "Oh, by the way, Colonel Wilkins, I wonder if you've seen Lieutenant Prescott around? Kenneth Prescott, you know. He was stationed on Governors Island, too." But perhaps Colonel Wilkins wouldn't remember, or had never met such a lowly person as the second lieutenant, and she would have to catalogue further, "Well, he's tall and has sort of a big nose, but not too big, sort of thin and aristocratic looking; and blue eyes that are crooked—I don't mean crossed or anything, they just start out straight then droop, with kind of a cute, sleepy look; and he has neat, sort of nothing-colored hair that shoots up in a double cowlick." Oh, no, she couldn't do that. Ken Prescott was nothing at all as she had described him, and it would sound silly to add, "And he's handsome and—and intriguing."

Tippy sighed and went on spooning up her soup while the dull girl beside her talked of teaching school and hoped she would be able to teach in one of the schools for army children in Germany. "Not in the one I have to go to," Tippy prayed silently, trying to see if an officer who had his back to her was equipped with a double cowlick. Peter Jordon's photograph was in her purse, under the white napkin on her lap, and the image of him was in her mind, just as clear and unfaded as when he had told her good-by; but her eyes traveled over the dining room and her heart lifted with the thought that, since Peter couldn't be here in person, it would be nice, it would be *very* nice, if Ken Prescott should happen to be around for ten days.

CHAPTER II

THE ship plowed steadily through the waves and its passengers settled down to a life as monotonous as the throbbing of its engines. Tin trays clattered at five o'clock in the morning; the public address system routed people from their cabins with its calls of "First sitting," . . . "Second sitting," and left those who ate at the last tables to come as quickly as their duties permitted, and either to sit in relaxed peace or bolt their food and return to work. During the day it transmitted messages, filled the entire ship with commands for the chief engineer, the chief carpenter, or the transport commander to report to the bridge; and at noon on the first day, when the befuddled passengers were just beginning to learn where they lived and were still surprised to have chosen the right deck, the right corridor, and especially the right direction to their rooms, it spluttered for a moment, then blurted out:

"Attention all passengers. There will be a fire drill at two o'clock. At the sound of the gong, passengers will don their life preservers which will be found in the wall rack beside their beds, and will remain in their staterooms until the second gong is sounded. Enlisted men will report to their lifeboat crew or fire hose station. At the sound of the second gong, passengers will file in orderly procession from their cabins and will stand on deck at the station indicated on the chart which will be found on each stateroom door. They will line up against the wall, keeping the deck clear for lifeboat and fire crews, and will remain so until the all clear, or final gong is sounded. All passengers will be required to attend. All babies in arms and small children will wear their life pre-servers. Repeat:"

Tippy was at lunch when everyone stopped talking to listen to the message, and when the clink of dishes began again she said, "My soul, I don't see how some of these people will ever make it. The ocean's as calm as a cup of consomme, but a lot of the people have turned pea green and some can't get out of bed. Why do you suppose they have it so *soon?*"

"It's routine on a transport," Colonel Wilkins told her. And then, he added seriously, to the whole table, "The Russian situation in Berlin is tense, so we may have several drills. A friend of mine told me that on the last transport coming home, the officers were alerted all the way. Every precaution was taken, from Bremerhaven through the English channel and out into the Atlantic. Not that trouble was expected," he added. "They were only being watchful."

"Do you—do you think we may have war?" Mrs. Parrish asked the question hesitantly, as if she voiced something she had feared to face, but her look brightened when he told her:

"I don't think so, not for some time, at least. Our air lift is working and looks as if it could carry on; our country is beginning to wake up to danger and the need for prepared-ness, so I should say we may be able to hold it to a cold war. It doesn't look as tough to me as it did in July. What's your opinion, Max?"

Colonel Caldwell looked startled and yet so pleased to be consulted, that Tippy realized he rarely was asked for an opinion, at least by his wife and daughter. He sat up straighter, picking up his fork and laying it down while he talked, and since the discourse she had started showed signs of lasting all through the meal, Tippy let her mind wander off on reflections of its own.

A fire and lifeboat drill should bring Lieutenant Prescott out into the open, she thought, provided he actually *was* on the ship. It should send him charging along the decks, his long legs covering ground and his ridiculous hair battened down by an overseas cap. A second lieutenant should be just about the correct rank of officer, being the lowest, to act as policeman to a bewildered flock of sheep. So she ate her lunch and was glad when it was time to return to her stateroom and try on the bulky contraption which was designed to save her life in a crisis.

"Good grief, child, what are you doing?" her mother asked, when she came in and found Tippy buckled and tied into a grease-smeared canvas vest and perched on a chair.

"I'm ready." Tippy lifted her chin like a turtle poking its head out of its shell, and Mrs. Parrish laughed.

"Without a coat?" she commented. "It would be mighty cold taking to a lifeboat without a coat, and it won't be any too warm just standing on deck and playing makebelieve."

"I hadn't thought about that." Tippy tugged loose her straps, put on her heavy tweed coat with its fur lining, and looked even more like a turtle. "There," she said, sitting on her mother's bed when she found she couldn't fit in again between the arms of the chair. "I wish it were time."

"You still have fifteen minutes until the first gong, which won't be for us." Mrs. Parrish sat down to read a magazine and Tippy waited in hot discomfort.

But at last, not only a gong clanged with reverberating fervor but the ship's deep horn accompanied it, and Tippy poked her head through the porthole and watched the deck outside become as busy as any Main street on Saturday afternoon. Soldiers poured from exits, fire hoses shot streams of water back into the sea, and a lifeboat that had been swung out from above came jerkily down into view. From his bridge, the ship's captain bellowed orders to his sailors over an amplifier, terse and sharp. Feet pounded along the deck, crews shouted, counted off, then the lifeboat was jerked up again and all was still.

"Well, it's time for us, now," Tippy said, pulling in her

head and grinning at her mother as the room was filled with a second clamor. "That sure is a becoming costume you're wearing."

"Isn't it? Let's go."

They opened their stateroom door and joined the parade of puffy figures filing past. Everyone moved quietly. Some were silent because they were under orders and were endeavoring to do their best, but others were too sick to care. The smallest children looked like white marshmallows because their little life preservers were new and clean, and many a mother's back ached from trying to hold a fat cocoon against her own bulky, padded front.

"Here, let me hang onto your little boy for you," Tippy said to one who leaned weakly against the wall and seemed uncaring that her child was screaming his lungs out. "He's frightened."

"Uh." The poor girl closed her eyes and gave limp surrender of a small clinging hand while Tippy forgot she had planned to search the officers who charged past, and knelt down.

"We're just having lots of fun, darling," she explained, wiping tears from a round little face and smiling into terrified brown eyes. "We're playing a funny game. We dressed ourselves up in these funny suits and we're playing like we're great big soldiers or sailors. Would you rather be a soldier like your daddy, or a sailor?"

"Sol. . . ." The Captain's voice cut off the end of his word.

"Passengers dismissed," he shouted. "Crew ten will remain at its post. All enlisted personnel will repeat drill immediately. Time must be cut by two minutes. Lieutenant Prescott, report to Colonel Mears."

So, thought Tippy, while her heart gave a delighted bounce, he *is* on board! There was no time to dally and watch for him, or even to stroll toward the transport commander's suite, for her small new friend was plastered against her and as she stood up she lifted him, too. "I'll carry him back for you," she offered. "Or if you'd like me to, I'll entertain him for a while."

"It's his nap time. I think that's what upset him, not being able to go to sleep and knowing something was wrong with me. I hope I feel better tomorrow."

"Oh, you will." Tippy grinned at the girl and helped her along the corridor. "I'm never queazy, myself," she said, feeling a little smug and pleased with her sturdy constitution, "but I know lots of people who can't even look at a rowboat. Is this where you live? Well, if I can do anything for you let me know. I'm in B-7."

"Oh, thanks, but I'm sure I can manage now. Two other girls are in with me. Our husbands are sergeants and I don't suppose we'll see much of them during the trip, except at meals and for an hour or two in the evenings. The girls can help me, but thanks for what you did."

"I was glad to." Tippy gave the marshmallow a kiss and passed him over; then she pranced back along the corridor, enjoying the roll of the floor beneath her feet. She was beginning to enjoy the journey, and since her mother was lying on the lower bed, reading, she climbed to her top bunk, repacked her life preserver into its rack and was slipping quietly out of the room again, when Mrs. Parrish looked up and asked:

"Now, where are you going?"

"I thought I might sit on deck for a while. It's wonderful up on top where the lifeboats are and, do you know, the whole place is covered with deck chairs! They appeared this morning, good, sturdy ones, so that we won't need the canvas contraptions Bobby and Alcie brought us."

"No, but bless Bobbie's heart for thinking of them; and they did have only benches yesterday." Mrs. Parrish smiled fondly at two orange-and-green chairs that were folded and stacked in the corner with the big cases, and added, "It was darling and thoughtful of him, and we'll put them in our garden next summer. I can sit and look at the mountains and think of him."

"Sort of like sitting on his lap." Tippy opened the desk and took out a new leather portfolio filled with air mail stationary, and decided, "I guess I'll begin my diary to Alcie. I may forget half the stuff I want to tell her if I don't put down a little every day. Not that there's much, yet, to tell her, except about the fire drill and that we've had three good meals and can go to the movies tonight."

"All right, but don't blow off into the sea."

"I won't."

She found a secluded spot where she could watch the prow of the ship as it marched through the waves and gave a bob now and then as if in polite obeisance to the sea, and since she was quite alone and had nothing to look at but water, she wrote two letters. One began:

"*Alcie, my pet:*

"*He is on board! I haven't run across him, yet, but I'm bound to meet him sometime, don't you think? With my usual luck, I'll probably be in the middle of some silly predicament when it happens, so I intend to be on the look-out and stay as dignified as I can. I almost jumped right out of my life preserver when I heard his name called over the mike. Penny said he was on here but, gosh, I couldn't believe her. It's going to be frightfully exciting to see if he hunts me up (I suppose I should say, if he hunts up Mums and me.) I'll keep you up to date on everything that happens.*"

And the other one began:

"Dear Peter:

"We have been on our dull way for twenty-four hours. Nothing of interest to report. We had a fire drill. The food is good."

Tippy capped her fountain pen and slid farther down in her chair. People were waking from their delayed naps and had begun mid-afternoon promenades, and she watched them through heavily drooping eyelids. "Oh, my goodness to Betsy," she suddenly muttered, "imagine me being sleepy in the daytime!" and swung her legs from the footrest and jumped up. "I can sleep at night," she told herself, grinning ruefully, because, with the trip scarcely started, she was already tired of having Tippy Parrish for her only companion. "I might go and ask somebody to show me some engines, so I can write Bobby about them. Or perhaps the P.X. is open, or I can find *something* to do."

She marched off along the deck and in the course of her wanderings discovered a small glass-enclosed room at one end of the lounge. It held an upright piano, and a girl about her own age was playing such masterful music that Tippy opened the door to listen.

"Oh, that was marvelous!" she cried involuntarily, when a run and two crashing chords ended in silence. "I'm Tippy Parrish, and could I come in and listen?"

"Sure, come in." The girl looked around with a careful smile that, tight-lipped as it was, disclosed a double row of braces on her teeth. She had nice hair, black and naturally curly, but added to the braces was a pair of harlequin glasses. "I'm Martha MacCallister," she answered, hesitant and with her fingers going back to the keys.

"You surely can play." Tippy crossed the room to lean on the piano and the girl nodded.

"Yes," she said, showing neither gratitude nor pleasure, "I'm studying to be a concert pianist. Do you like jive?" And

[30]

without waiting for an answer, her strong, sure fingers struck the keys and danced up and down them in a medley of chords and rhythm that started Tippy's shoulders moving and brought two boys and a girl to the door.

From that moment on, Martha MacCallister became the ship's Pied Piper. She could bring youth on the run more quickly than gongs got them to their meals, and could hold them in the little glass-enclosed room against the call of the sun and in spite of a storm that sent them skidding across the floor while they danced. And because of her, Tippy wrote to Alice Jordon on the fifth day:

"Well, it happened. I met him yesterday. And like I said it would be, I was in a mess. Martha was playing the piano and we were dancing, or at least we were trying to dance with the boat going in every direction but forward. Dick Kemper (he's the nice red haired boy who is going to Vienna) was flinging me around in a kind of adagio number we were working up for the ship's concert (if they have one) and I looked up and there he stood—practically staring in the door. My shirt tail was out of my slacks and Dick had thrown me right in his face. (Ken's face, I mean.) There was just a piece of glass between us and I couldn't think of a thing to say. I just panted. But he opened the door and stuck his head inside—as far as he could get it with me in the way— and said, 'Hello, Tip.' And oh, Alcie, I looked so awful!"

Tippy sighed and stopped writing as she thought of her embarrassment. Everything would have been all right, she reflected, if Martha had stopped playing like a maestro and had minded her mother. The record player would have given out slow, measured music for decorous dancing because most of its platters were Strauss waltzes, and Tippy knew she

[31]

would have looked very attractive gliding about the floor with her print skirt billowing. It was the adagio business that had lured her into slacks. But, she admitted honestly, Martha was never a popular partner when the record player was called into service. No one could blame her for clinging to her importance on the piano bench, especially after Mrs. MacCallister had looked in and chided sweetly, "Darling, *please!* No more popular music today. You're ruining your touch. Now remember, Martha, no more. Only the classical." And with that she had closed the door and trotted back to her bridge game, sure that her dutiful daughter would obey her.

Martha's beautiful afternoon would have fallen in ruins. Neither Dick nor Rod Archer would have asked her to dance. Anyone could see that Rod was her idea of the perfect athlete, hero of the gridiron, and pert Sharon Reilly would have taken him up to the top deck to play shuffleboard. So, satisfied with a grin now and then instead of a partner, Martha had waited only until her mother was safely out of hearing and had begun to play again, faster and more invitingly than before. And Tippy had changed from her best print dress into slacks. Clad in rags instead of riches, she now reflected bitterly, a pitiful Cinderella who stayed too late at the ball, and who had perspiration running down her face in streams. "Boy, it was that last split and getting jerked up like a kite that did it," she groaned, biting her pen.

But whatever it was, she had shot through the air like the man on the flying trapeze, straight at Kenneth Prescott, Second Lieutenant of Cavalry, Armored. Or even worse, she tortured herself further, she must have reminded Lieutenant Prescott of an old Sherman tank plunging into action.

The casual greeting she had received did nothing to rebuild her complete disintegration or the embarrassment of having to wipe her face on her sleeve before she could see his outstretched hand. He had waited courteously, like an

amused but patient statue. And when she eventually put her
fingers in his grasp, she made a bridge that pumped up and
down and seemed permanent.

"How are you making out, Tip?" he asked, while she
prayed for release.

"Just fine." Her high school class ring bit into her fingers
and all the charms on her bracelet were flying around like pin
wheels, and she was furious with herself for adding, "We
were wondering if you made this boat." "We" might have
meant her mother, but the flush that turned her cheeks from
a fading pink to a bright carmine plainly told that it didn't,
and she made hasty introductions of the staring four behind
her.

Ken Prescott answered them with four nice nods and a
steady grin, and without giving her back her hand, suggested, "How about finding your mother with me? I've been
wanting to pay a call on her but I'm kept so darned busy that
I never have a minute to myself. I'm just the lowest ranking
errand boy on the ship. Didn't you hear me get honorable
mention over the loud speaker after the fire drill the other
day?" And after waiting through her mute stare, he went
on, "That was just to prep me for the fourteen additional
things I'm to remember next time."

His drooping eyes looked too lazy to remember anything
at all until one noticed how blue and keen their pupils were,
but his over-anxious hair was always alive and eager to be
out in front and Tippy decided he was both calm and efficient.

"See? I've got a note book," he said, when they were outside, producing a small black book with his free hand. "I
bought it new for the trip and it's already half full."

Tippy didn't mind his holding on to her, now, although
she felt like a puppy on a leash. He swung her hand as if he
were glad to have found a young companion, as if he, too,
were homesick and a little lonely. But she asked hesitantly,

"Ken, would you mind going on up to the top deck and finding Mums while I sneak into our stateroom and change? I feel so hot and messy in slacks."

"Why? You look okay to me."

"But the slacks. . . ." She stopped and explained, "They bunch up funny around my waist."

Without meaning to, she had called attention to a part of her anatomy that was her mother's despair. Any skirt was always too large for Tippy's waist and had to be altered. And Ken looked at the encircling red leather belt and said, "Gosh, there isn't much of you, is there? I could put that thing around my neck for a collar." The top of her head came just above the insignia on the shoulder straps of his battle jacket, and he repeated again with wonder, "Gosh. Am I so tall or are you so little?"

"Some of both, I guess." She answered with a laugh, and quite unconscious that he was seeing her for the first time as a girl, a very pretty girl who was old enough for dates and not one just to be teased, as he had done on Governors Island. "I have on ballet slippers and they haven't any heels," she added, thrusting out a foot.

Ken looked into her serious hazel eyes thoughtfully. "You surprise me, cherub," he said, pulling her along again. "Keep on your slacks, you're cute in 'em, even if they do bunch up. But I'll take you to the movies tonight if you'll put on a dress. How about that white job you wore at your birthday party? The night you reached the grim old age of sixteen."

"But that's an *evening* dress," she protested, laughing. "You don't wear a formal on an army transport."

"Okay, then we'll settle for something simpler. But it's a date, huh?"

"It's a date."

Tippy sat thinking it over and wondering how she could write it all to Alcie.

The first part would be easy, especially if she kept her mind on her misery, but how to toss in, casually of course, that he had stopped pulling her along and, instead, had linked their arms together while they marched gayly through the corridors, quite like a grown-up couple. And he had called her "cherub." Cherub was Penny's pet name for her. Penny always said it with a sweet caressing lilt that made it a name to be desired; and Ken had done a very good copy of her tone. Too good to describe to Alcie.

So she scowled down at her paper and finally scribbled, "*I guess that's about all. He did ask Mums and me to the movies last night, but Mums had promised to play bridge so I went with him. It was a very good movie.*"

CHAPTER III

"Tippy, can't you put this contraption away?" Mrs. Parrish pointed at the open desk where a new portable typewriter took up most of the room, adding significantly, "You never use it and all I do is stumble over its case."

"Well, I guess I could, although I'd planned to write a story for Josh. He gave me the typewriter so I could write stories, you know." Tippy looked up from tying her shoe and grinned at her mother's next words.

"In two days? My child, you've had over a week in which to write a story, and you're never still long enough to write even a letter. The few you've managed to scrawl have been done on deck and you let the one to Penny blow over the side of the ship. Today will all be taken up with watching the coast of England and tomorrow we'll be going through the Channel and packing and. . . ."

"That's enough, friend." Tippy jumped up, whisked the typewriter off of the desk and said with it in her arms, "I really planned to relax on this trip, to be dull and further my career as an author; and here I am, plumb worn out. I'm tired."

"Well, why don't you stay still for five seconds? I never see you except at meals and to bow to when we pass in the corridors. Some of us take naps, you know, and rest and read."

"No can do." Tippy was bent double, fastening clasps and locking her case, and she went on, "We worked like dogs, practicing for that ship's affair that didn't come off. I think it would have been a lot more interesting to hear Martha

MacCallister play and watch Dick fling me around like a feather pillow than to have a baby contest. Who gives a whoop about a *baby* contest? My soul! And Mrs. Raymond was going to sing, too."

"Honey, Mrs. Raymond absolutely refused to sing and Martha did play for us one night."

"Yeah, before a bingo game, when everyone was counting out beans and hunting a good card. That makes me mad." She set her square case in a corner and added with a sigh, "I guess the dancing's over, though, for Mrs. MacCallister simply haunts the sunroom and won't let Martha even touch the piano. Poor Mart, it's about the only fun she ever gets, except the movies. You know," she leaned against the desk and said thoughtfully, "I wouldn't want to make a child of mine always be so serious and always thinking about her future. Martha's never done anything but practice for hours every day, ever since she was a little bit of a girl, because she's going to be famous sometime. What earthly good is it to be famous," she asked, "if you don't ever have any fun getting to be that way?"

"Music takes work, dear," her mother answered, and added slyly, "and so does writing."

"Yip, that I know—to my sorrow." Tippy's ardor was no more quenched than a bonfire after a teacup of water had been poured on it, and she retorted amiably, "But I'm still sorry for Martha. I know I kicked up quite a fuss when I decided to be a writer, and I may still be one—when I get around to it. But I think I'll do it the way Penny got to be an actress, sort of take it easy and trust to luck."

Mrs. Parrish had to laugh. It pleased her to see Tippy apparently happy and over her homesickness, and since her emotions were always unstable, were either soaring like a bird in the sky or pressed as flat as a fallen leaf underfoot in the rain, she asked mildly, "What's on your agenda for to-day?"

[37]

"Well," Tippy thought that over while she scratched her ear. "I'm signed up for shuffleboard this morning," she said, "if those two beastly little boys don't get up there first and grab the court. And, of course, I'm going with you to the Captain's coffee party and to watch the radar and look through the glasses at England and see how everything works on the bridge. That ought to be fun. And tonight's the last movie and Ken thinks he can get off in time for it. In between times. . . ."

"Ken isn't working as hard, now, is he?"

"Nope, not since things got in better running order, but he says he'll have to be up most all night tomorrow night, checking troops, you know. He's nice, Mums."

"Yes, I think he is." Mrs. Parrish took her stationery from a pigeonhole in the desk and glanced at Tippy's thoughtful face. "Penny always thought he was a very sweet child when he used to visit at Fort Arden. They used to let him tag along with their older crowd."

"Well, he's old, himself, now." Tippy stood considering Kenneth Prescott. Her head nodded up and down as if she were deciding something within herself and she said, "But I'm not scared of him like I was. He doesn't make me feel silly. But, of course, that might be because I haven't Bobby along to always put me in some stupid situation. Every time I used to see Ken, Bobby was making me act like an idiot, and I never could talk with any sense. I can, now. I can talk to him almost as well as I could to Peter. Funny, isn't it?"

"Yes, honey, perhaps it is, to you. But after all, you're sixteen and should be able to talk with a man who is only six years older. I don't suppose Ken feels so ancient."

"I don't know what he feels." Tippy flapped her hand in a wave of dismissal to Ken and pushed away from the desk. "But I do know, I'm going to miss that court if I don't get under way." She went to the door but stopped with her hand on the knob to say, "If the subject of our discussion should

[38]

show up here and looking for me, you might tell him where I am. He's kind of a lonesome soul and there isn't a single girl his age aboard, except that Caldwell creature. Or you might give up a morning with your buddies and take him in tow. 'By."

She sent back a wave, let the door bang shut and followed the turns in a maze of corridors. Only two more days were left before a new life would reach out and claim her. The ship had become dear and familiar, like a large even-tempered fish that would turn around and swim back to America. The life before her was a dragon. A dragon with its dark cavern of a mouth wide open, waiting for her to walk between its sharp, bared teeth, into captivity. Tippy had discussed the dragon with herself and wanted to postpone her meeting with it as long as possible, to push away even the thought of it, and so had filled every hour of her days with mad activity.

"Oh, golly, I'm glad I wasn't a Pilgrim," she said that evening to Ken, when they were leaning on the rail, watching the lights of a great liner pass them as if they were standing still.

"Why?"

"Because I'm not the adventurous type. I don't like going off to strange places to live or braving dangers to make a new life. I'm just a home town gal who thinks my country is super. Right or wrong, it's my country and I'm satisfied with it."

"Perhaps that's because it happens to be a good one," he returned, finding her more interesting than the distant ship and leaning back on his elbows to watch her. She was a cute little moppet, he thought, with her perky, straight nose and the dimples that popped in and out every time her mouth twitched. "Perhaps you're statisfied with your country because it has always been good to you, Tip," he said. "You may love it even more when you see what others have done to their people."

[39]

"I don't want to see." And then she told him about the dragon. "It's gobbled up all the people in Europe," she ended, not caring whether he understood her, or if he laughed and thought her a little crazy. "And it's waiting to gobble up me. But I'll fool it."

She looked so fierce standing by the rail, so like a determined pigmy going into battle, that he laid his hand over hers. "Tippy," he said gently, "don't be so tense about everything. You're always buckling on your armor and charging out to fight something."

"What do I ever fight?"

"Mrs. MacCallister, for one thing. Ever since you've been on this ship you've defied Mrs. MacCallister. You egg Martha on to play instead of work and I shouldn't be surprised to see you yank off her braces before we land."

"I did get her glasses off, for a while," she admitted sheepishly. "And Martha could see fine. She wouldn't have to wear the darn things if she wasn't always bunched over and staring at music." Tippy stuck out her neck and hunched her shoulders to demonstrate Martha's posture on a piano bench and Ken was glad to feel her fingers relax under his, although she went on: "This is the last fun she'll have for ages, because the dragon will sure be after her. He'll feed her to every *Musik Meister* in Germany and will chain her to a piano. You wait and see. What else have I fought?"

"Lots. Yourself, part of the time, and. . . . But tell me first, where did you get this dragon, this horrible monster who rules Germany?"

"I thought him up. Or perhaps he came to me. I don't know where I got him." Tippy leaned over the rail again and her hand moved from under Ken's to snuggle inside the cuff of her coat. "I just get to thinking things sometimes," she said.

"So you cooked up a great big monster and you're planning to kill him, all by yourself."

"I don't think I'd have much chance of killing him," she answered, "but if he doesn't get me first, I may damage him a little." And then she sighed and shook her head. "I guess you don't understand," she said. "You just think I'm being funny and talk a lot."

"I do understand, Tip. It may sound crazy to say it, but I do. I even understand well enough to ask you a question." He waited until she turned her head to look at him and then asked, "Have you ever thought of fear as a monster?"

"Fear?" She considered the word, then blinked her eyes and repeated, "Fear? Do you mean I'm afraid to go to Europe? Afraid of war, or something?"

"No, cherub, just afraid of change. Of living differently, of being with strange people, of. . . ."

But Tippy shook her head. "I'm not afraid," she said, "not when I'm with Mums and Dad. I know Dad will get us all out if war happens. No," she sighed, troubled and groping, "it isn't anything quite like that, and this is the nearest I've ever come to finding out *exactly* what it is. It hit me when I was about to get on the boat and made me cry so hard on Penny that I couldn't walk up the gangplank. Oh, it's just a silly old dragon," she decided, trying to laugh. "When I meet him, I'll let you know."

"Promise?"

"Of course. I'll call you up in Munich and you'll hear a weak little voice saying, 'Help, help, help.' " Tippy piped the words in a squeaky treble that made them both laugh, and made Ken say:

"You're a lot like Penny, cherub. Once I told you you weren't, but I've changed my mind. Penny was always full of fancies, and ups and downs."

"Well, she turned out to be an actress so perhaps I'll be a writer. It would be swell if I had enough ideas inside of me so that I wouldn't have to work to think up any, wouldn't it?"

The passing ship was far ahead of them now, its lights

mere dots in the dark, and squinting at it, she asked, "Shall we make the eight o'clock movie?"

"If you think you've talked yourself out."

"I have, and you've been awfully patient. I'd have told me to go jump in the ocean." Tippy turned away from the rail as Ken linked his arm through hers. "I don't get this way very often," she explained. "And I don't talk about it to anybody except. . . ." She hesitated, and he leaned down to tease:

"Except to Peter Jordon?"

But she shook her head. "I was going to say, Trudy," she answered. "Trudy always understands. She knew just how much I wanted to grow up enough to be called '*Miss* Tippy,' not plain 'Tippy,' and she always figures out why I'm in a muddle. Peter's nice," she added, "but we don't ever seem to get on silly subjects."

"What do you talk to Peter about?" They had reached the door to the lounge, and as he held it open for her, Ken wished he could brace his arm across the opening, could block it and watch her expression. But she answered his desire by turning her head and smiling at him.

"We talk about West Point and—things," she said, her hazel eyes shining gold in the light. "You know, dates and the gang, and what we're going to do tomorrow."

"But when you have serious thoughts and need advice, you'll come to me and let me be Trudy, won't you?" he asked, thinking that he sounded like a kind old uncle addressing a favorite niece, and feeling a relieved return to youth when she said:

"Of course. But you're kind of young, yourself, to know very much."

And that was the last he saw of her until the ship was tied to the dock in Bremerhaven. Once he waved to her across the lounge, when she was coming out of one dining room door and he was hurrying in the other one, but he had troop duties on his mind and a night's work ahead of him.

The harbor was filled with gay little pleasure launches as the transport steamed into it. Americans were out to welcome their countrymen and they called greetings while their boats skimmed over the water like bright little bugs. A cutter waited, rocking on the waves, until the ship slowed and they could meet. Then, with passengers crowding the rails to watch, a ladder was lowered and army officers from Bremerhaven's Port of Embarkation climbed aboard.

"My goodness, Tippy," Mrs. Parrish cried, "that was Colonel Jackson who just got on! I declare, I'm getting so excited!" She leaned out to look down at the cutter, then up at the low, green shoreline. "Isn't it beautiful, and wouldn't it be wonderful if Dad would come to meet us?" she said, swallowing hard to get out the words.

"Umhum, but don't be too hopeful, Mums. Dad's a long way off, you know, clear across Germany."

"And how big do you think Germany is, my pet?" her mother retorted, moving over a few inches to let a little boy squeeze in beside her. "It would take a day and a night from Garmisch, at the most, and I've known him to rush from California to Philadelphia to meet me. Oh, we're going right on past the dock! Look at the cars and the *people!*"

The dock at Bremerhaven is merely a brick and concrete platform built on the shoreline. A railroad track runs its length between low warehouses, and a long gray road skirts a water basin and a partly demolished navy yard. Ships were tied up along the dock. There was another transport waiting to sail for home and two Victory ships unloading cargo. Tippy looked enviously at the ships as she went past them, then turned her eyes on an open space where men in American uniforms rushed about or waited and watched in groups.

"I don't see Dad with that bunch of officers," she said, "but here comes an official car and two more sedans. One of them looks kind of like ours."

[43]

"But it isn't." Mrs. Parrish shook her head and waved with the rest of the passengers.

Everyone waved. The troops sent a concerted cheer across the narrow strip of water. Then the slowly moving ship stopped. For a moment it shook with the power of its mighty leashed engines, before waves churned and it began to back. A small tug steamed out and valiantly pushed it toward the dock while two giant cranes trundled forward over the brick to meet it. The cranes carried gangplanks as if they were straws and came to a halt near the water's edge. Interested passengers got in the way of hurrying sailors; children lost their parents and screamed lustily; a baby's cap fell overboard; and small boys raced up and down along the decks, poking their heads between the grown-ups in a vain endeavor to see. Ropes were flung out. The giant cranes moved again and stopped. Doors in the ship's hold opened. A section of a rail was removed, and the gangplanks swung out and over.

"Well, here we are," Tippy said, as if remarking on rainy weather, and watching the crowd stream back into the lounge. "What happens, now?"

"I don't know." Mrs. Parrish tucked strands of escaping hair under her hat and gave the group of officers on shore one more thorough search. "Someone told me we must declare our dollars and change them into scrip," she said, eager for the next step that would bring her closer to her husband. "I'll go inside and find out how we do it and you stay here and keep an eye out for Dad. I feel sure he'll come."

"All right."

Tippy smiled at her mother because she knew how excited Mrs. Parrish was, but when the deck was hers again, she turned and leaned on the rail. Far in the distance she could see a town. It was beyond the basin with its neat array of anchored ships, beyond a low line of trees and sandy hills, and it looked drab and gray. "Bremerhaven, I suppose," she muttered to herself.

"Right. You're a smart girl."

Without turning, she knew it was Ken, and she said, "Oh, hello. Are you all through working?"

"I'm on my own now," he answered happily. "I'm just a casual."

"What did you do with your men?"

"Turned them over to the fellows who'll take them in charge. They're to go all over Germany—Heidelberg, Frankfurt, outlying constabulary posts, and some even to Vienna. Most of them are replacements for troops coming home," he explained, "and they'll get travel orders and be on their own. How about you?"

"I don't know. Mums has gone to see about us."

"A lot of seeing she's doing," he remarked with a grin. "Right now, she's sitting around the table in Colonel Mears' office with three very nice-looking gents, drinking a mug of coffee."

"Mums is?" Tippy stared, and asked, "Is Dad with her?"

"Nope." Ken shook his head, then inquired, teasing, "Does he have to be when she has a date?"

"Of course not. But she told me to stay here and watch . . . she said she would go in and get us some money so we could get off." Tippy looked so puzzled that he set her mind at rest by explaining:

"Your mother's a gal who's been in the army a long time and knows a lot of people. The first one she ran into was Colonel Jackson, and he took her off to see a couple of more high-ranking birds who took her off to have coffee with them; for it seems they've been on the dock since the cold wee hours of dawn and needed it. She was as excited as a chipmunk and snagged me down on her way, craftily telling me where she had left you and suggesting I break it to you that you'll be fatherless until around noon tomorrow. It was a pleasure, I assure you," he added hastily, when two narrow lines appeared between her eyes; but she only asked:

"Then Dad isn't coming?"

"He can't. The Port has a rule that people can't see their relatives off or come to fetch them, because they haven't any place to stay. The whole town was bombed to the ground, you know, and there's only one big hotel where out-going families are kept and processed for sailing. If they broke the rule and let even one person come, they'd have to break it for a thousand. So your father sent a letter by Colonel Jackson and said he'd meet you in Munich. That's where I leave you," he added, "so I'll take you that far and turn you over to him."

"Why, thank you very much. You make me feel exactly like a prisoner being transferred from one guard to another." Tippy tried to laugh, but her heart wasn't in it, and she put her arm around a white post and leaned against it as she asked, "How soon can we start?"

"Well," Ken hesitated. He looked into her clouded eyes and wanted to warn lightly, "Watch out for that dragon," but he knew it was a poor time to be facetious; so said in a voice that matched her mood, "there's still more to this prisoner business. You can't get off the ship until evening."

Her mouth dropped open and stayed that way, even while he hurriedly explained further:

"You see, army trains leave here in the evening. They have to, in order to get to places at the right time, because it's a long way down from the coast. They go at five, six and seven."

"And what do we do in the meantime?"

"Just what we've done for the last ten days: eat and mill around."

"Can't we even get off and take a walk? Can't we even walk down the gangplank?"

[46]

"Nope, not till train time. The trains are moved up, right over there on those tracks, and we walk over to them."

"Well, my soul." Tippy thought she had seen the army at its most efficient best. Such amazing organization as this never had been presented to her before, and she acknowledged it by saying, "Gosh." And then adding with honest acceptance, "I realize that this is different from just moving troops. You've got children to figure on. I suppose if you let families get off and stroll around, Junior might crawl under a switch engine or some dumb family would be sure to go too far and not get back in time. I guess it's better to keep us under control."

"But you're one of the lucky ones," he told her, unable to tease her longer. "The Port Commander sent passes for you and your mother, and you're both to drive in and lunch at the club. Colonel and Mrs. Jackson are giving a luncheon for your mother and asking the army people she knows who are stationed in Bremerhaven."

"Are you going?" Tippy let go of her post and straightened up. "Are you invited, Ken?" she asked again, her eyes wide with the anticipation of release. But at his negative headshake she settled back again. "I don't think I want to spend a morning and all afternoon with a lot of older people," she said, "unless. . . ." A sudden idea popped into her mind and she dashed across the deck to the lounge door, calling over her shoulder, "Don't go away. Stay right here." Then she stubbed her toe on the high sill that was there to keep water out of the lounge when decks were swabbed and the sea was rough, and with her sandaled foot clasped in both hands, groaned, "Ouch. Colonel Jackson, oh, ouch . . . was David's godfather. I know he'll want you to come to lunch and . . . oh, *dear!*"

Ken went across to peer between a web of suede straps at her injured toes, and when they had decided no bones were broken, he said, "I can't go. I haven't a pass, Tip."

[47]

"He'll fix it." Tippy winced with pain as she put her foot down, but she straightened her brown suit skirt, set her dot of felt hat on straight again, and said, with her hand pressing on her chest, "You know, I've just hurt so much here, this morning, that it almost feels good to hurt somewhere else. Please don't go away."

"I won't."

Ken walked back to the rail and looked down at all the activity. Trunks and boxes were coming out of the hold. They were being trundled along the ramp by Germans, young boys with flopping hair that was worn too long; by old men who were stooped. Soon the cars would roll out, American cars that Americans must have. American clothes, American cars, he thought, trade mark of an industrious people.

Ken was proud of the scene. He was proud of his compatriots who brought their electric gadgets with them, their refrigerators, sanitary wire screening, and washing machines; who bought and planned for comfort. "They live—*right!*" he silently told the crates. "They're what makes America good. And even if it costs a lot to get the stuff over here, Uncle Sam wants them to have it. He wants them to stay used to *good living.*"

Unlike Tippy, he was eager to be a part of the scene before him. It was his first real job, his first chance to prove himself as an officer in the United States Army; and he was impatient for evening to come, impatient for tomorrow. And above all, he was impatient to see the ruined city where he would help bring order out of chaos.

CHAPTER IV

TIPPY was very quiet on the drive in to Bremerhaven. She sat on the back seat of Colonel Jackson's car between her mother and Ken, while Colonel Jackson, who was in front with his soldier driver, pointed out sights the others found interesting.

Miles of road ran from the dock to the main gate of the port. It curved past the basin with its anchored ships, through a flat busy area of barracks and guards; and after passes had been checked and military police had saluted the car past a sentry box, Colonel Jackson said, "We're going through the old section of the town and a part which, due to being a strategic military target, caught the worst of the bombing.

Tippy looked at block after block of ruined buildings. Nothing she had seen in the newsreels or magazines had prepared her for this. Whole apartment houses were roofless shells full of gaping holes which had been windows. Now and then a sagging floor showed through; and sometimes a section or even a room could still be used and had people living in it. There was nothing but rubble in what once had been the main business section of the town, nothing but bricks and plaster cleaned away so pedestrians could walk on the broken sidewalks. And in a park of green trees the front of an old brick church still stood, its steeple pointing hopefully skyward.

"The raid lasted twenty minutes," Colonel Jackson said, "and thirty thousand people were killed. In Castle, which you can see from the train as you go through, it lasted half an hour and thirty-five thousand died."

"Is—is all Germany like this?" Tippy asked, looking at the people in the streets and knowing his answer would mean very little to her because she would have to see for herself.

"The greater part of it is. The cities, especially, and any part that had power plants or factories, or railroad terminals. But we've done a great deal toward cleaning it up."

Tippy watched all the people who went their way along narrow streets. They were neat and clean, but the women still wore dresses reaching only to their knees and short, tight-fitting coats and thick, cheap stockings. The men looked better, though their suits were old and frayed, and now and then an army overcoat had turned civilian. Little children played along the curbs as little children always will, not caring that their clothes were either washed to a faded drab or sleazily new under their coarse knitted sweaters. Everyone walked in worn, scuffed shoes, for bicycles and an overcrowded street car were the only means of transportation. Short and high, the street car clanged and rattled along the cobbled street; and when it stopped at a corner, such a crowd surged toward it that passing was impossible and Colonel Jackson motioned his driver to go another way.

"The rest of the town is better," he said, smiling into Tippy's stricken eyes. "Not so much damage was done out there and our club will make you think you're at home."

"I wish it could," she whispered to Ken, under cover of the questions her mother was asking. "I keep thinking, what if this had happened to us?"

"I know. But it didn't, Tip," he whispered back. "We won."

"Of course we did. But what if we shouldn't, sometime? Lots of people thought Mums and I were crazy to come over here and take a chance on our lives. They wanted us to stay home where it's safe. What *is* safe," she asked, "with war as awful as it is?"

"Nothing," he answered. "Not one darn thing except

thinking straight and doing the best we can as individuals and a nation. And keeping smart and our eyes open!" he added.

"I guess that's right." She settled back to look at a park and long streets with beautiful homes. Now and then a house was missing or was partly destroyed, but trees and shrubbery grew thick around its ruins and would remain brightly fresh and green until their leaves dropped off for winter. So she made an effort to repay her host by saying, "Colonel Jackson, this is an interesting drive."

And she was thankful that the club was gay. Uniforms were everywhere. Women, looking very smart, rushed at Mrs. Parrish with outstretched arms, and after the first glad welcome, wailed, "Your skirts *are* longer than ours. We knew they would be."

Tippy liked the club because it was a little bit of home, and hated to leave it. But their passes were good only until three o'clock, and the time came when she had to climb the steep gangplank again, back to her shipmates who were becoming restive under waiting.

"Honestly," she said to her own special friends, finding them in the little room where Martha had broken rules and was playing the piano again, "if you think you're discouraged over staying on the ship all day, just wait till you see all I saw. It's perfectly unbelievable."

"What's it like, Tip?" Dick asked.

But she only shook her head and frowned at Martha's glasses that were back on her nose. "I thought you were going to leave those off," she scolded. "It's perfectly horrible, Bremerhaven, I mean; and you'll see it from the train because we go right through it. What time are you all leaving?"

Some would be on the five o'clock train, some the seven, and only Martha would start at six with Tippy and her mother. "Oh, good," Tippy said to her. "We'll have fun, maybe—I hope—because Ken Prescott will be with us and a couple of other lieutenants he knows, but you'd better not let me catch you wearing those specs. Not when you're sitting down anyway. You can see fine, sitting down." Martha tried a grateful tight-lipped grin, and she admonished further, "And smile naturally. Your braces don't look so bad, do they, Rod?"

"I never noticed 'em." Rod was trying to show her the new paper money he had received, but he turned to Martha and said gallantly, "I didn't even know you wore 'em." Then, having done his duty, he held out a fan of paper. "That's a nickel," he explained, taking out the smallest piece which was about half the size of an American dollar bill.

"Well, for goodness' sake." Tippy took the paper five cents while she sent the happy Martha a grin that meant, "I told you so," and asked, "What's the rest of it?"

She put out her hand, palm up, and he laid small oblongs of paper on it, one at a time, saying, "This one's a dollar. This is five bucks and it's the largest amount I have, though Dad got some for ten, twenty, and even fifty and a hundred. This is ten cents, and here's one for a quarter and one that's fifty cents. Some fun, isn't it?"

"Golly, I hope I won't get all mixed up." Tippy fanned out the money as he had and studied it before she gave it back. "Where do we spend it?" she asked.

"In the Post Exchange, dope," he answered. "And in the Commissary and hotels and restaurants. We can't buy in any place that isn't run by the Government."

"I know that and there isn't anything to buy, anyway." She gave back the money and told them, "I saw the stores. There isn't anything in the stores. Most of them haven't even glass in front. Colonel Jackson said the proprietors put out what little they have to sell every morning and take it home with them at night. He said. . . ."

"That won't trouble us because the Post Exchanges are full of things." Rod pocketed his money again and asked her,

"Did you go down to the ship's P.X. and buy the two cartons of cigarettes you're entitled to?"

"Well, of course I didn't." Tippy drew herself up and looked indigant. "You know, perfectly well, I don't smoke."

"Sure, but you've got to have cigarettes to tip with."

"Tip what with—whom, I mean?"

"Germans. That's all you use over here. Look." He had attended a meeting the night before that Tippy and her mother had missed, and he prepared to brief her on her future in Europe. "A German carries your baggage," he said, sitting down on a small leather and chromium sofa and pulling her down beside him while the others gathered in an interested group, "and you have to pay him. Right?"

"Right." Tippy nodded solemnly, and he went on:

"So what do you give him? He can't use American scrip and you haven't any marks. They wouldn't be any good to him even if you had them, because they won't buy anything. So what do you do?"

"I give him cigarettes," she answered promptly, feeling pleased with herself. And then she had to spoil it by asking, "But why? Don't they even have cigarettes to smoke over here?"

"They don't smoke them, they trade them around. Cigarettes are money to the Germans. They buy food and clothes; and if a family hasn't cigarettes or chocolate or tea, it doesn't eat."

"But what happens to them in the end?" Tippy could see one cigarette passing from hand to hand, spilling out its tobacco and becoming more limp and dirty with each transaction, and she asked again, "Who gets them when they're practically done for?"

"Search me." Dick put in his opinion and shrugged as he said, "That's what I want to know. It looks as if the manufacturers, or the farmers, or the black marketeers can just sit back and puff all day. Somebody must get them unless they keep on going like a chain letter."

"Well, whatever becomes of them," she suddenly decided, "I'd better have some to start out with." She jumped up but stopped at the door to ask, "Can you still buy them with dollars?"

"Sure, as long as you're on the ship."

Mrs. Parrish was just leaving a corner of the lounge where two officers sat behind card tables, exchanging American money for American scrip, and Tippy skidded to a stop beside her. "Oh, Mums," she cried, "I have to buy some cigarettes —for tips, you know, not to smoke! And we must get our dollars changed!"

"I've done it, honey," her mother answered, patting her purse, "and I bought our allotment of cigarettes this morning before the P.X. closed its doors. You're a little late, aren't you?"

"I guess so, but I didn't know all the things we had to do till Rod told me. Where did you learn so much?"

"Over my coffee this morning. Let's close our bags and be ready when our turn comes."

Tippy and Mrs. Parrish walked along the corridor together and it was only a half-hour later when they were startled by a knock. "I'll answer it," Tippy said, and opened the door to the room steward's bright Filipino grin.

"Time now you go," he said, motioning beyond her to the locked luggage. *"Gepäck Trägers,* they come."

"Who?" Tippy peered around him and saw three stalwart German boys in the corridor. "Oh, the porters," she translated, opening the door wider so they could file past her. "We *sind.* . . ." She looked helplessly at her mother, then pointed. *"Hier,"* she ended, grinning with pride that two words had been remembered from the lessons David had tried to give her, even if one was pronounced like its English equivalent. And she added for polite good measure, *"Danke schön."*

"Bitte schön," they answered solemnly, picking up the heavy cases and leaving her on the end of her conversational rope.

Mrs. Parrish was trying to multiply the correct number of cigarettes each one should receive by three, and when she had settled on a pack-and-a-half and had dispensed them, Tippy startled her by ripping open her purse and thrusting another package at the last man to go out the door. "Why, Tippy Parrish," she cried, do you know how much money you gave them?"

"No. How much?"

"Between us, we gave them about thirty dollars. That's some tip just for carrying a few bags across a platform and putting them on a train."

"It is, isn't it?" Tippy ducked her head in rueful apology at her mother's next words.

"Cigarettes are rationed," she said, "and Dad and I do smoke, you know. Your carton-and-four-packs a week will be all the extra allowance we'll have to count on."

"Well, I'll tell you what I'll do." Tippy considered the cigarette problem one of the minor ones to be solved in Germany, and offered, "I'll save the butts for you. I'll collect all the nice long butts every morning and. . . ."

"You can't," her mother interrupted, "because the servants get the butts. It's a part of their wages. And they get the coffee grounds, too. Myra Jackson told me there's always a pot of coffee on the stove and a box of grounds being dried out, and no one ever, *ever* drops a cigarette on the ground and steps on it. The Germans take out the unburned tobacco and save it. And people will come right up to your car and ask to empty its ash tray."

"Oh." Tippy picked up her coat and went silently out of the room. Here was one more horrible thing the dragon had done, she thought. It had taught people to be cringing beggars.

[55]

The sun was setting as she crossed the brick dock beside her mother. They skirted a partially destroyed railroad station and stepped over tracks that had been re-laid since the war. The long train that waited beyond, looked exactly like pictures she had seen of European trains, in that the sleeping cars were low to the ground and had small compartments with big windows, through which the luggage was shoved. It looked like a picture postcard on the outside, with the people standing in their little rooms or leaning out through open windows; but when Tippy stepped from a platform into the vestibule, the resemblance ended.

The train was old. It was battle-scarred from war and falling apart. Its floor was concrete, broken and repaired in many places; and in the long corridor, bits of rubber still clung to a strip of brass binding. The walls were a dirty dull mahogany and the light was so dim that an officer who stood just inside with his chart had to use a flashlight to find the number of their room.

"There you are," he said, wrenching open a sagging door. "Your stuff's all in. Okay?"

"Okay." Mrs. Parrish smiled and nodded. And when he had rushed off to his duties, leaving a white-coated German porter standing in his place, she said haltingly, as Tippy had done, "*Ist . . . gut.*"

"Thank you, *madam.*" The little German puffed out under his coat and his lined face formed a polite smile. "If you desire anything, you will seek me out, yes?"

"*Ja.*" The "Ja" came out to her great surprise and as the result of having mentally rehearsed a conversation and any answers she might have to make, and she hastily repaired it with, "Yes. *Danke*—I mean, thank you - er - a —thank you, very much." Then she quickly slammed the door and said to Tippy who had the giggles, "I'm so confused I don't know which language I'm trying to speak. Anyone would thin¹⁻ I certainly could speak my own. But I went to the German class on the ship and we all practiced so hard that . . ." She broke off to ask, "Do you suppose we won't have to speak German, after all?"

"I imagine most of the people we'll see have learned English from the occupation forces and have been chosen to work for us because they can speak it," Tippy answered, dropping her coat on the neatly made-up bed and adding, "The good old army blanket is still with us, I see. Golly, the place looks so dirty I hate to touch anything."

"It isn't dirty, honey," her mother comforted, trying to squeeze past her and wondering where their luggage could be. "It's just old. Where do you suppose that door goes?"

"Try it and see. *Ja?*" Tippy sat down on the olive drab blanket and laughed again, since laughing was better than bursting into tears, and watched her mother give a feeble tap before she turned the doorknob.

"Oh, I guess we have this room, too," Mrs. Parrish said, looking into another dim cubicle. "Our bags are all in here and another bed is made up. Now, isn't that nice!"

"I'll take it. I don't mind stepping over stuff." Tippy maneuvered past her mother, staked out her claim to the second room by putting her toilet case on the bed and taking off her gloves.

Twilight was darkening the scene beyond her window and blurring the figures running to and fro. The *Gepäck Trägers* had finished the train load of Americans and were riding away on their bicycles. The engine gave a silly little toot, a high peep that not only meant it was about to be on its way, but was promptly taking off, and the wheels began to move.

"Next phase," Tippy muttered, going to stand in her door.

It seemed important to see the dock once more and her ship that could return to America. The train rolled slowly as she crossed the corridor and stood at an open window. There's my stateroom, she thought, counting the portholes as she passed them. The room I didn't want. The clean lovely

[57]

room that had the feel of America in it. Some of her friends were still standing beside the rail, waving. She fluttered her hand with the rest of the people who were crowded into the corridor and leaned out as far as she could when the train swung around a bend and went off in a wide curve toward Bremerhaven.

"Well," she said with a sigh, when there was nothing more to see, "willy-nilly, Germany, here we come."

"And how!" Ken was turning up unexpectedly, as usual, and he sounded so pleased, so almost fatuous, that she faced him with a smile. He held a bottle of her favorite soft drink and she said, all in one breath, "You sound as if you're tickled a beautiful glowing pink. Where did you get that?"

"From a guy who came around with a cart, just like the ice cream man at home. Have a swallow." He held out the bottle and added as she took it, "They tell me you'll see carts in all the big stations along our way, and all you have to do to get one is lean out the window and wave a paper nickel. I'll bet it's an eye-opener to the Germans and makes them drool. Too bad the Russians can't see the way the American army travels: every soldier in a nice clean bed in a clean little room."

"Clean?" Tippy looked down at the floor, then gave the bottle back. "I guess it is," she said, not wanting to spoil his enthusiasm. "At least, you can bet we do the best we can with what we have."

But he only took the bottle and stood shaking it back and forth, watching an inch or so of brown liquid bubble up. The grin had left his face and she wondered what was going on behind his slanting eyelids as he looked down at the swirling bubbles. And at last she had to ask, "Do I sound horrid, Ken?"

"No, but you aren't doing the best with what you have. You talk about America, but, my gosh. . . ." He broke off, took a last swallow and set the bottle on the window sill.

[58]

The train was swinging around the end of its arc through the ruined outskirts of Bremerhaven; and after watching shattered, deserted buildings for a moment, he turned and let his grin spread slowly. "I guess I ought to tell you, Tip, that I was thinking about you last night when a little man came into my room. He was kind of a little gnome man with a long gray beard and a peaked cap, and he sat on the rim of my porthole for quite a while, just talking things over, and he said to tell you that the dragon doesn't live in Garmisch. He knows the dragon, and he said to tell you he doesn't live there."

"He—did?" Tippy moved away from the destruction outside and leaned against the corridor wall. "He sounds nice, your little man," she said. "Does he live in Garmisch?"

"Sometimes. He always used to live way up on one of those peaks of the Zugspitze, but he says he travels around a lot, now. He's been in the Rockies and in the Andes, and down in the hills of Tennessee, but he says he likes the Zugspitze best. He's seen wars come and go, wars, ruins, peace, rebuilding; and nothing ever touches Nature. The old Zugspitze just stands there as strong and calm as she ever was. She has her whole family around her and they just stand there and look down at Garmisch in the valley. They're so strong that the dragon didn't come to Garmisch."

"Did he—did he tell you what the dragon is, Ken?" Tippy looked up hopefully but he shook his head.

"He said *you* would, sometime," he answered. "He said you'd find out all about him; that he's just a bunch of hot air and only scares little people. He said you'd probably kill him deader than a door nail and then you'd tell me about it." Ken watched her hazel eyes that were a liquid gold, so deep that one could look and look and never see to the bottom of them, and when her lashes swept down to hide them, he wondered if she knew her dragon was a personal belief, chained to her and dragging along wherever she went. More like a pet

[59]

cur, he thought wryly, slinking along behind. Then he added, "He said he'd watched you and, if you wanted to, you sure could make a swell dragon fighter."

"Oh." Tippy drew in a long breath and released it in a sigh. "You—you talk a lot like Trudy," she murmured, rubbing one thumb nail against the other and watching the break it made on her nail polish. "Thank you, Ken."

"You're welcome. Want to go in to supper? We've got a swell diner on and every meal costs forty cents in our new paper money," he remarked lightly, to change the subject. "And it's a good time to practice your German."

"All right, though we'll probably speak English." She stepped inside her door for her purse as the train pulled into the remains of Bremerhaven's station.

It was quite dark now and nothing could be seen outside her window, but she squared her shoulders, and with a defiant jerk of her head, said into the night, "Okay, Germany. Here *I* come!"

CHAPTER V

THE trip to Munich was uneventful except for the sight of devastation to be seen all along the way and the discomfort of having no running water. Soot poured in the open windows because the late September day was warm and they were pulled down from the top. Passengers wanted to look at bomb-shattered houses and small truck gardens where Germans industriously harvested their crops, so sat forward on the worn upholstered sofas that had been their beds and became so spotted with black freckles that they looked as if they had some dire disease. The corridors were constantly full of people bearing paper cups of water from a tin tank by the door, and handkerchiefs were used as wash cloths, and bits of cleansing tissue were thrown out of the windows to float away on the wind.

Martha MacCallister and her family left the train at Augsburg. And after Tippy had told her good-by with a comforting promise of letters and visits, she filled two cups with water and carried them in to her mother. "It isn't very long, now, till Munich," she announced, poking Mrs. Parrish in the back as she leaned out of the window, still hoping to see her husband on the platform. "I don't know about you, but I'm going to scrub myself and change my blouse. Here, take this."

Mrs. Parrish drew in her head and turned around. "Thanks," she said. "I just keep wishing Dad could get nearer than Munich to meet us."

"You've been looking for him ever since we left Heidelberg. He told you he couldn't, pet. See you later."

Tippy carried her cup into her own small room and closed the door. She kept up a determined whistle while she scrubbed her neck and ears and cold creamed her face. She tugged a blouse out of one of the cases and, upside down and fastening the locks again, muttered, "You little old man of the mountains, you," then stood up and went on with her whistling.

I helped Marty, anyway, she thought, going off key while her mind wandered. I sent her on to Regensburg with a bang and a zest. She said she wished she could be as happy and sure of having a good time as I am. She said she wished she were *exactly like me. Well!* This last compliment was worth considering, and her whistle trailed off into silence while she sat down on the sofa and stared at the wall. "Hm," she said aloud. And then again, "Hm."

She was still sitting, her blouse in her hand, when the door opened and her mother peered in. "We're almost there, honey," Mrs. Parrish said. "Have you been looking out?"

"No. Why?" Tippy put her thoughts away until a later date as her mother answered:

"Munich's in ruins. There isn't anything to see that isn't a mess. It's so terribly depressing. It's. . . ."

"Now, don't you say that. We're over here to fix it, aren't we? We have the Marshall Plan, and we're trying to help everyone." Tippy jumped up and slid into her blouse. "Listen," she said, almost forgetting her mother, "I'm beginning to see something. I'm beginning to see."

"What?"

"I don't know." She tucked her blouse into her skirt and pressed her lips together in the way that made her dimples flicker. "You concentrate on Dad and I'll concentrate on some personal business I have."

The train was pulling into the ruins of a great station. Noon sunshine filtered through a twisted steel dome which, before the war, had been a glass umbrella against rain and snow and was now but a useless burned-out skeleton; and she tugged at her window strap. The glass went down with an obedient bang and she leaned out as far as she safely could. Her mother's head was in the window before her, and in a sudden burst of joy, she searched the long platform.

Germans, waiting in stolid patience for their own trains, turned to stare at her. They stood among their boxes and bundles, in their pitiful clothes, and stared without envy or even curiosity. Many of the men wore leather shorts and long knitted socks, and had knapsacks strapped to their backs. One father was giving his little boy bits of food from a battered suitcase. They squatted down on the brick together as the father took out each bit carefully, hungrily watching the child as he ate it. Tippy's eyes found them, then looked unhappily away and watched the platform again.

Luggage was being shoved through other windows and she called to her mother, "If Dad isn't here, shouldn't we get off, anyway?" But Mrs. Parrish shook her head.

"The train goes on through Garmisch," she answered, still looking far ahead. "He said to stay on till he meets us."

"And that might land us in Vienna." Tippy straightened up to rest her back, and then, over the other heads, she saw him. He was striding along with his cavalryman's walk that always had a little roll in it, as if he were riding a horse, and even as fast as he came, his eyes were searching the windows. He looked so good to her with his military cap at just the correct angle over his graying hair and his dear, strong face so eager and excited, that she waved both arms and shouted, "Yoo-hoo! Yoo-hoo! Oh, Dad!"

"Where is he? Oh, where is he? Oh, dear, me!" Mrs. Parrish cried, trying to see, too. "I can't find him."

"He's on the train now, silly. He saw me and got on." Tippy left her window and ran to Mrs. Parrish's, to draw her in and straighten her hat. "You're some sight for an arriving wife," she said tenderly. "Hold still, there's soot on your nose again." She felt like the motherly one, scrubbing away at an

[63]

impatient child, and had given only one dab when the door burst open and two strong arms enclosed them.

"Oh, gosh, my girls!" Colonel Parrish said. His arm held Tippy against him but his cheek stayed pressed against his wife's, and he repeated, over and over, as if he could never say it enough, "Oh, Marge, Margie. Oh, Marge."

"I know, Dave. I'm here."

Tippy stood quietly, knowing her father would remember her in a moment, and smoothing the woolen sleeve of his uniform. This was why no hardships mattered to her mother, she thought. This beautiful, sustaining love was greater than anything else in the world; and in a great burst of tenderness, she suddenly whispered, "Oh, I love you both so much." And then they remembered her.

"Hi, youngest," her father said, giving her the last kiss he had left over. "Where did you come from?"

"Well, originally from the land of the free and the home of one not too brave," she retorted, "but I've been standing here for quite some time. Is there any danger of this contraption going off and taking us with it?"

"No, but we have to shove the luggage out." Colonel Parrish released them both and plumped his wife on the sofa so he could see out of the window. "Hey!" he shouted. *"Bitte! Du! Bitte!"* Then he turned around and grinned. "Those are all the words I know," he told them comically. "Nothing's happening."

"Here, let me." Tippy squeezed in beside him and took one look. "Oh, good morning, Lieutenant Prescott," she said to the face that was looking, quite conveniently, in to hers. "How about lending us those *Gepäck Trägers* you have in tow?"

"I brought them for you." Ken flashed her a grin. Then, because she was much too triumphant over her accomplishment to think of introducing him to her father, he spoke to

Colonel Parrish. "I'm Kenneth Prescott, sir. I used to tag around after Penny at Fort Arden."

"Well, glad to see you again, boy. And thanks for bringing porters. Have them stand by and I'll hand them things."

"You'll do nothing of the kind." Tippy came to and explained, "He got wounded in the war and he hasn't any earthly business lifting anything heavy."

"Coming in." Ken's long legs covered ground and Colonel Parrish tried to make his keen blue eyes look round and innocent.

"Well," he inquired, "may I ask what brings on all this swell attention?"

"You may ask but you won't find out a thing." Tippy knew she was blushing like a sunrise and so retreated to safety in her own cubicle. "You two love birds can go on," she offered in exchange for privacy. "I'll help Ken."

She listened for some return, for the rumble of her father's voice asking questions, but when none came she knew they had gone outside. Then she was busy with the luggage. She relayed small pieces and scrambled out of the way when Ken lifted a big case and shoved it through. And in a few moments they were walking toward what once had been a handsome station and was now but a vast room with the sky for a roof; she and Ken in front, her parents a contented couple behind them.

"How is our youngest making out?" Colonel Parrish was asking, watching Tippy's little brown hat in its curly tan frame bobbing along ahead. "You wrote that she didn't want to come, but is she any better about it?"

"I don't know." Mrs. Parrish tucked her arm through her husband's and clasped his hand with hers for comfort. "Sometimes she seems as happy as a child," she answered, "and is all bubbling enthusiasm; and then, the very next minute, she looks as if someone had struck her or stolen her favorite doll.

Tippy is such a strange child," she sighed. "She's so much more *complicated* than the others."

"Penny was 'complicated,' too, if you remember," he returned, smiling a little. "But she didn't grow up in a time when there was so much to be complicated about. Life was simpler before the war and our horizons were narrower. Penny had eighteen pleasant years in which to get adjusted, remember that."

"I do." Mrs. Parrish looked at Tippy ahead of her, smiling up at Ken, and said unexpectedly, "She's getting quite tall, isn't she? Almost as tall as Penny. Somehow, I always think of her as little."

"It's the silly heels women wear," Colonel Parrish answered, bending down to see what his own wife had on. "You're quite a little girl, too, Margie, when you stand on your own two feet. And you'll be glad to do it when you start tramping up and down the hills of Garmisch."

"Is it pretty?"

"One of the loveliest and quaintest spots I've ever seen. It's a picture postcard town. All the houses are tucked around on hillsides, on crooked roads that have lots of mud puddles and no sidewalks, and they all manage to have a view of the ring of mountains. And they're built of white stucco and brown-stained wood, with beamed eaves that are wide enough to make a roof over all their balconies. They're all decked with balconies and have pictures painted on their sides. Some even have decorations painted around their windows. One old hotel —golly, you'll love that hotel."

"What is it like?" she asked eagerly.

"It has windows painted on and painted people looking out of the windows. And its near a stream that goes wandering around through the town, an ice-cold mountain river that tumbles over rocks and under bridges. Whenever you ask an officer how to get to his house, he always says to cross one of the bridges and take such-and-such a road up a hill."

"And our house?"

"It's a dandy."

There was no time to say more for they had reached a door that wasn't really a door, but only a great hole, and Tippy and Ken with three porters were waiting on a large plaza. Tippy was looking uphappily at two of the porters who had leather straps across their shoulders. The heaviest cases were hanging from the straps and, bent and awkward under their burdens, they were waiting there as patiently as pack mules.

"Oh, for goodness' sake, let's *do* something!" she cried. "I thought you were never coming, the way you strolled along."

"Our car is parked right over here," Colonel Parrish hurried to answer, suddenly as concerned as she was and leading the way. But he asked over his shoulder, "Can we give you a lift, Prescott?"

"No, thank you, sir," Ken answered. "They told me in Bremerhaven that my hotel would be right across from the station. I'll trot on over."

"Oh, yes, the Excelsior. It's for Americans and it's right there," he pointed. "Across from what's left of that big department store. Well, come down and see us whenever you can."

"Thank you, sir. I just told Tippy that my car should be along on the next boat. It didn't make this one," he said, opening the door of the Parrish's sedan and arranging the luggage on the back seat so Tippy would have enough room. "I bought it second-hand a day or so before I left and couldn't get it to the dock in time. It's a convertible," he added, proud of the first possession he had bought with his own pay.

"What Gran calls a 'collapsible.'" Tippy offered, excited, too. "And it's a nineteen-forty seven model and simply covered with gadgets. Radio and 'frog lights'—Gran again—and everything. Ken's going to drive down next week and. . . ."

[67]

"Well, get yourself in here or you won't be home in time," her father admonished, proffering the porters their ration of cigarettes, which was four apiece, and turning to grin at his wife's startled stare. "That is the correct amount, Mrs. Parrish," he said, in answer to her unspoken question. "I don't doubt that you paid them an exorbitant price in Bremerhaven, because I did, too. But we learn. This is a very correct, dollar apiece tip."

"Thank you, sir, for the lesson." She took her place in the car, waved to Ken Prescott, and watched Tippy settle into her own accustomed spot.

It seemed almost natural for the family to be starting out in the long, gray car, and except for the different scenery, it was like almost any trip they had taken across the American continent. Tippy closed her mind to the ruins of Munich, just as she had done on the train; but when Colonel Parrish stopped the car, she gazed down with the others on a great plain where once thousands had massed to pay homage to Hitler. Sheep grazed there, now. Three flocks of sheep, complete with shepherds and dogs, nibbled at the short grass, while children ran up and down the steps of the impressive monument he had ordered built to his greatness and where he had stood to demand obeisance. Hitler was gone. His magnificent estate of Berchtesgaden was a rest home for soldiers. The Nazis were gone, too, and Americans lived in their houses. The order of things had changed, and now little children played and sheep grazed contentedly.

Tippy thought about that while she rode through Munich. She wondered how it would feel to have arrows painted on your house, pointing the way to a bomb center; to be always ready to run, and to have the arrows used as markers for rescue squads should they have to dig you out. She wondered about all the people who trudged beside the country road, too, along the neat footpaths, carrying loads of branches strapped to their backs; and about those who rode bicycles and had bundles and knapsacks tied on behind; and those who pulled heavy carts of wood with very small children trying to help. Sometimes she saw cows hitched to ox carts, thin sad cows that looked as hopeless as the man who drove them; and several times her father had to creep slowly up a hill behind a rattle-trap car that had a stove built on the side of it. There was no gasoline, for Germans, and the car was chugging along on its wood-burning contrivance.

People rarely noticed the fine American car with its Army of Occupation license and it was as if the Parrishes were ghosts riding past them. Only the horn woke them to life and scattered chickens and dogs and children from the streets of villages it passed through. And suddenly, Tippy was lonesome. "Dad," she said, sitting up and breaking into an earnest conversation, "how much farther is it to Garmisch?"

"We should see the mountains any minute, now," he answered. "We would have, long before this, if it weren't so hazy. There's a gap in the mountains and we wind around through the valley a bit, then. . . . Marge," he broke off to say, "we'll go right through a tunnel where Hitler made *Messerschmitts*. When things got hot, he assembled them in there and darned if we could find them. I guess we never thought of looking down here," he added. "We didn't do any bombing in this section of the country below Munich."

"Well, I'm glad of that." Tippy sighed and sat back. "I'm glad I won't have to look at horrid, ruined buildings every day."

"You'll live in a scene as peaceful as a painting," he told her. "And except that we have plenty of Americans there and a swell time, you'll think you're back in the good old days of the Passion Play, when Oberammergau was a religious center and Garmisch and its twin city, Partenkirchen, were the play resorts of the rich. And, Marge," he turned to his wife again to say, "even right now, the hotels are full of rich Germans, black marketeers, probably. We let the Germans keep some of the hotels and one of the biggest ski runs and an ice rink, and they're having themselves a time. Golly, you'll love it here. Just the air makes me feel so good I want to climb the Kreuzeck and ski down to glory."

"Fall down to the hospital," she retorted. "Look, I see the mountains."

"Umhum. And see that tall point over behind the lower ones? That's old lady Zugspitze. She's the highest peak in Germany, but I've got a jagged old fellow I like better, myself. Oh, boy, it's good to have you here!"

He shot the car forward with an extra burst of speed and it seemed no time at all until they had sailed through Hitler's tunneled factory and were rolling past a golf course dotted with scattered players. "Ours," he said. Then he leaned out to call, "Hey, Bill! I've got 'em!" And explained, when two clasped hands shook a congratulatory wave, "That's Bill Macklin. His wife's been a whizz at settling us in, and they're coming over tonight. They've got a kid Tippy's age."

Tippy wanted to ask what sex the "kid" was, but there were too many interesting things now to see. The town had begun. It had begun with small white houses and a wealth of old trees. Flowers still flourished everywhere and spilled from boxes on the brown wooden balconies her father had described. A herd of cows was coming home from a day of grazing in the hills, their bells ringing cheerily as they sauntered along the street; and she was to learn that when the cows came home, traffic stopped. A car might have to halt a dozen times, because each cow knew its own road and when it was time to turn off, and made no fuss or confusion as it rambled away from the others. They knew their own lanes, their own gates, and were always on the wrong side of the street for a turn. "Cute," she said, loving the way they stopped to consider the car before they walked in front of it, and the moo they gave their ontrudging friends, a moo that plainly said, "Good-by. I'll see you tomorrow."

There was much too much to look at and Tippy's head bobbed from one side to the other. There was the narrow, neat river, always popping up unexpectedly, and the hotel with its painted people. Houses perched on hillsides amid a gayety of trees and flowers and painted walls, and she asked, "Dad, have we a painting on our house?"

"Yep. It's a big picture of a man and boy with a pair of scales, and they're weighing bales and boxes. I think the Nazi people who lived here were in the shipping business, but . . . well, you can look now for yourself."

He swung the car around a corner where ground flattened out and lawns were wide and fenced, and Tippy had her first view of a long, and very high, white house.

At first it seemed all brown balconies and roof and shining windows; then she saw a wide, tiled terrace above a semi-circular rock garden. Her eyes had found a small projecting sunroom and a small portico at the side of the house when a young man leaped down the rock steps from the terrace and along the graveled drive. He swung the gate back with a flourish and a series of double bending bows that were a signal for four women to appear on the portico.

"Thank you, Jochen," Colonel Parrish called, and added to his wife, "There's your staff."

"All those people?" Mrs. Parrish looked at the boy and waiting German girls before she got out of the car. "What can I say to them?" she whispered.

"Shake hands with them," he answered, grinning and enjoying her misery. Then he added soberly, "Do you think you could say 'Grüss Gott' to each one? It means 'God's greeting to you,' and is the custom down here. You say it every time you leave home for five minutes or have a night's sleep."

"I'll try." She stepped timidly out of the car and smiled at five beaming figures who were now lined up along the flag-stone walk. And when Colonel Parrish said, "This is Hilde,"

[71]

she held out her hand in a friendly way and said, *"Grüss Gott,* Hilde," meaning it with all her heart. And *"Grüss Gott,* Annie. And Bertha, and Maria. And last but not least the young, bright Jochen, with his flopping hair and Colonel Parrish's double-breasted gray flannel jacket and blue polka-dot tie.

Tippy recognized the jacket as she followed behind her mother and gave her own greetings, and she thought it was lucky for the maids that Parrish women had come, for their dresses looked like the ones she had seen in Bremerhaven and Munich, faded and above their knees. She knew of one print in her trunk which would almost fit the smallish Annie and had already selected several of her mother's for the other three.

Then she was conscious that Mrs. Parrish had gone up the steps and was standing with her hands clasped while tears spilled out of her eyes. "Oh, how sweet, how thoughtful!" she cried, staring at the door until Tippy dashed up to see what had made her mother weep when nothing on the trip had been able to shake her.

The door was trimmed in a garland of green. A wreath of flowers made a frame for a hand-painted card on which was lettered, in every color of the rainbow:

WELCOME WIFE
WELCOME DAUGHTER
WELCOME TO GARMISCH

HERZLICH WILLKOMMEN

"It was their idea," Colonel Parrish said. "It's their greeting to you, and they've worked all day on the door and paid an artist to paint the sign."

"It's lovely." Mrs. Parrish turned on the small portico and held out her hands again. "Oh, thank you, so very much," she said slowly, hoping they would understand. "I know we're all going to be happy here, together. I will be very happy, and I want you to be. My daughter. . . ."

But Tippy squeezed forward, too. German words of thanks had come to her and she smiled shyly before she tried to use them. *"Danke,"* she said carefully. *"Viele Danke."*

CHAPTER VI

LIFE in Garmisch had begun. It had been under way for exactly twenty-five hours, sixteen minutes and thirty-five seconds, and Tippy sat in the living room and considered it. The living room was really three large rooms joined by wide arches and furnished with comfortable chairs and heavily carved mahogany pieces reaching almost to the ceiling. One piece had a serpentined front and, flat as a book case, was made up of tier after tier of little drawers that were ornately inlaid with other woods; and when she wasn't watching the tall clock in a corner she counted the drawers. She usually came out at one hundred and seventeen but sometimes her mind wandered and she had to start over.

The mountains were massed in silent guard beyond the window and behind her, and at last she tired of the drawers, the clock and a painting of sheep, and exchanged the sofa for a deep, upholstered chair that faced them. "Oh, me," she sighed, folding her hands in her lap and staring at the snow-capped peaks.

Up to now, time had managed to saunter along. To be sure, its gait was no prancing gallop but, like a stroll in the park, it had provided mild entertainment and certain interesting sights. The house had been inspected, from servants rooms on the third floor to immense kitchens in the basement. Tippy had been impressed with the grandeur of her bed room, and the fact that, with all its fine furnishings, it had a wash basin in it. She could find her way all over the house, now, through the wasted space of serving pantries, pressing room, sewing room; could make the circuit without opening any wrong doors, and knew the German girls apart and what each one did.

Stolid blond Hilde cooked. At least, she did the best she could for a person who had grown up during the war and so never had seen a fine cut of meat and was unaccustomed to using even so much as a small stick of butter. Maria was the housemaid and had a frizzy permanent and was often attacked by a nervous fit of giggles. Her English and Tippy's German usually brought on the convulsions, so they had ceased to talk to each other and simply confined themselves to making signs. Bertha was the wispy laundress who lived at home with her husband, and who, even when she had nothing to wash, would come every day and receive three meals. And Annie; Tippy liked Annie best of them all, although she had no job and only came along with Bertha to help where she could, because she was hungry. They were all young, but Jochen was the youngest and was the problem child.

"I don't wonder you ask me why we have him," Colonel Parrish had said the night before at dinner, when Jochen was serving with a fine flourish that sent dishes skidding along a tray he had found in a drawer, and had stumbled over the rug on his run to the dumb-waiter. "I inherited the whole batch when I was living at the Schoenblick Hotel. Hilde and Maria were maids there and attached themselves to me when they heard I was setting up housekeeping. They said they'd find us a *Waschfrau,* and two came as the result. Jochen," he sighed, just as his energetic butler shot through the door again, and waiting until he had shot back out, "Jochen worked in the Schoenblick, too," he said, as fast as he could before another explosion emerged. "I told him there wasn't a thing he could do here, but the next morning he appeared with his parents. They're nice-looking people, by the way. The father's a doctor, but they couldn't feed Jochen. He's only seventeen, and is a big lad and growing too fast for the small rations they get. So they sent him up to work at the

[75]

American hotel, hoping he'd get enough to eat there, but sure enough, he didn't. Well," he concluded, "I couldn't resist the boy. He reminds me a little of Bobby, with his nice blue eyes and his big hands and always falling over things. But he's your department, now, Marge, and you can do what you like with him."

"We'll keep him, of course," Mrs. Parrish smiled fondly and wanted to mother the big willing boy who was trying so hard. "We'll keep them all, I suppose, though dear only knows how we'll pay them."

"We only have to pay two," her husband answered. "The German Economy pays Hilde and the gardener, Pavel. You didn't meet Pavel because I sent him to a doctor to have a cut hand looked at. The others get fifteen marks a month and their room and food. The *Waschfrau* wants to be paid in food to take home, and Annie. . . ." He stopped helplessly, then added, "I don't know what you'll do about Annie."

"We'll manage. If the commissary limits us on the amount of food we can buy, we'll eat less and share it." She looked across the table and smiled encouragement, because she knew he was troubled over his little flock and would have preferred to present her with more efficient servants. And when Jochen sprang in again, she said gently, "You're doing well, child. Don't run. We have much time."

And ever since then, one at a time and often in a chorus, the whole family had echoed her words, "Don't run, Jochen, don't run. *Nicht laufen.*" Tippy could say *"Nicht laufen,"* now, without an accent. It came out with the sight of her father's gray jacket flying through the hall, accompanied by a pair of shiny blue serge trousers and oversize Post Exchange shoes. They whizzed by, now, and even though they were behind her, she heard the racket and called absently, *"Nicht laufen, Jochen."*

"Aber Fraulein Macklin kommt!" he applied his brakes skillfully and thrust his broad, smiling face in the doorway.

He was happy that Tippy would have a young guest, and he announced eagerly, *"Sie wird bald klingeln."* A stabbing motion with one finger accompanied his words, and assuming he meant someone would soon be ringing a doorbell, she answered:

"Well, wait till she klingels. We mustn't look *too* anxious." But she got out of her chair and pulled down her pink sweater and smoothed her navy blue skirt.

Kay Macklin had failed to appear with her parents last night. "She is so terribly popular," her mother had remarked archly, enumerating all the delightful things her daughter did. So now, Tippy stood in the first of the three living rooms and regarded Kay anxiously. She was a tall girl with a pretty but petulant face. Her eyes were dark and her brown hair had been cut to fit like a cap, in exact and shining copy of an American fashion magazine. Colonel Parrish would have gasped at the height of her heels, and even Tippy was a little surprised at the swaying way she managed to walk on them. She suggested nothing of the outdoor girl, the sweater and skirt type whom Tippy liked, nor of the gay, fun-loving creature her mother had painted. "Hello," she said. "I had a few minutes and thought I'd drop in." And she fell into the first chair she came to and lit a cigarette.

Tippy hated to watch good money going up in useless smoke and hurried to supply an ash tray so Jochen could retrieve what was left of the tobacco. Then she sat down on the bench before a small upright piano, and they faced each other. "It's beautiful here, isn't it?" she said tentatively, and received a shrug in return.

Kay had already made up her mind that, as the only other girl in Garmisch near her own age, Tippy was an utter loss. The sweater and skirt and flat-soled shoes were enough. And without bothering about Tippy's face that many people thought even prettier than Penny's, or the graceful way she sat with her slender fingers clasped around one crossed knee,

[77]

Kay relaxed in the security of a social life unchallenged. "I suppose so," she said, "if you like to go hopping around the hills. I'm not the athletic type, myself, but the Casa's fun."

"Oh?" Not for worlds would Tippy have asked what the Casa was. And since she knew she would hear without delay, she waited.

"The Casa Carioca. It's the American night club. The music's good and the ice show's fair—for German skaters. I'd like it better, though, if people wouldn't always be dragging in their children. The enlisted men have it four nights a week and the officers only two, and Wednesday night is such a *family* night. It makes it rather disgusting, don't you think, to have children scooting all over the place?"

"Oh, yes."

"And then the German girls! Officers are always taking German girls there, and you bump into them on the dance floor and have to be polite when they come and sit down at your table. They come right over with the officers and sit down! That's stupid, don't you think?"

"Why?" Tippy had no thought of contesting the remark, she merely wanted to know. She could understand that it might be uncomfortable if extras crowded in where you were sitting, or difficult to converse in a foreign language; and, since each statement had asked her opinion and she had dutifully agreed with one, she felt entitled to a fair discussion.

But Kay frowned and said, "Well, of all the stupid questions! Are you pro-Nazi?"

"Of course I'm not." Tippy even laughed at that. "I just thought," she said, "living in a foreign country, it would be interesting to know the people."

"But not *girls!* Officers have no business to bring German girls to our dances."

"Well, they can't come alone." Tippy laughed at the spectacle of all the bachelors in Garmisch sitting silently together at tables while the married couples danced. But Kay cut in on her amusement by remarking acidly:

"There are a lot of other places they can take them. German places."

And that made Tippy think of Bobby. "I don't believe Mums would like that," she said, very softly, but with conviction in her tone. "I have a brother, Bob, and I don't think Mums would like him having to sneak around when he took a German girl out. If he couldn't find an American girl. . . ."

"There aren't any," Kay interrupted. "Your father and mine are the only colonels in Garmisch, all the rest of the officers are young."

"Well, then. . . ." Tippy knew Bobby would have to take *someone* to a dance. With the first toot of a horn he would have to be out on the floor and dancing; and since, not in a million years, would it be the grouchy piece before her, she said, "I suppose there must be lots of nice attractive girls in Garmisch. Goodness, they grew up the same as we did and they like to have a good time, too."

"I suppose so." The words were perfunctory and offered with a shrug, but Tippy persisted:

"It makes it kind of hard on the German boys, though, because they haven't any money and are always left out. Have you ever thought of that?"

"No, and it wouldn't bother me if I had." Kay's cigarette had burned to its end and there was nothing left for Jochen. "I'll have to run along," she said, crushing the few bits of tobacco into the ashes in the dish. "I have a date at five." And Tippy knew the visit had been a failure.

She thought of offering a compromise, even an apology of retreat, but only stood up from her bench. "I'm awfully sorry," she said, "but hope you'll come over again. Do you like to play golf? I'm not much good but we might go out some morning."

[79]

"I never played in my life. I freckle."

"Then we might try the American restaurant for an ice cream soda. I hear they're just like we get in the P.X. at home."

Tippy knew she had been rude. One didn't argue with a guest on a formal call or make an enemy instead of a friend. Kay had come to be admired; to be listened to with envious eyes, even to sponsor Tippy's social life and to offer up the least desirable of her suitors as a sacrifice. She had come reluctantly and at her father's bidding, but she had come. And now she was glad to be leaving. Her dark eyes snapped and she said:

"You're naive, aren't you?" And promptly tilted off through the hall with little time wasted in farewells.

It was interesting to watch the way she drove her car. A backward swish took her down the driveway and a spin of the wheel put her on the road; and Tippy stood on the little porch until she was out of sight beyond a tall hedge next door. "I sure muffed that one," she muttered, seeing her own family sedan turning in, and going down the steps to meet her mother and father. And then, like a naughty child, she poked her head through the car window and announced, "I dood it."

"What did you dood?" Colonel Parrish got out and came around to slip an arm about her waist. "Did you break any of the German furnishings we're signed for?" he asked, not at all anxious, since it was Tippy, not Bobby, who had been left alone among what had taken three pages to list as "valuable *bric-a-brac.*"

"I made Kay Macklin mad," she answered, stamping up the steps beside him. "But she made me mad, too. Honestly," she exploded, "she's the most disagreeable and supercilious girl I ever met!" There was a small wooden settee on the portico and she plumped herself down on it and faced both parents. "I haven't been in Garmisch but a day," she explained, "just one day, and I think I ought to have the right to make up my own mind whether everything is no good, or not. Kay is thumbs down on everything. *Nothing's* any good. Well, maybe it isn't, but I do think I ought to have the right to make up my own mind."

"You shall, my child, you shall." Her mother dropped a small package into Tippy's lap and consoled her, "It's French perfume I bought in the P.X. Sniff it and you'll feel happier."

"Thanks." And then she had to grin. "I feel just like I used to when you brought me a box of crayons from town," she said, "but I'm still mad. If Kay's the only girl I'll have to go to school with. . . ."

"She won't be, darling. She's eighteen and doesn't go to school." Mrs. Parrish reached for the door bell, saw Jochen looming up beyond the glass panel, and murmured as the door flew open, "It seems queer to keep our house locked. *Grüss Gott,* Jochen, and don't *lauf.*"

"And that brings an important question to mind." Tippy jumped up from her settee and did a good imitation of Jochen's long stride as she bounced into the hall behind her parents. "Where *am* I going to school?" she asked. "And when?"

"Ah, now it comes." Colonel Parrish dropped his overseas cap on a table and looked hopefully at his wife, but she became suddenly busy with her packages and muddled instructions to her puzzled butler. And when it seemed they would never stop gesturing at each other, he had to say, "Shall we all sit down in our third and best living room for a discussion of a problem?"

"Oh, yes. Let's." Mrs. Parrish turned to him brightly, even while she considered retreat down a long narrow hall which led from the square one in which they stood. It ran the length of the house and would get her beyond the last door to the living room and into the serving pantry before the others could go the long way round. But Tippy's troubled eyes were on her and she was asking:

"Has something gone wrong?"

"Of course not, lamb." She abandoned escape and led the way. "It's just this," she said, when they were seated and Tippy was on the divan and facing the hundred and seventeen drawers again. "There isn't a high school for Americans in Garmisch."

"Huh?"

There was no way to meet such a bewildered look and she explained hastily, "With only Kay Macklin's brother and two other boys old enough for high school, one couldn't be started. It was too expensive to bring teachers here."

"But what do they do about it?"

"Why they. . . ." Mrs. Parrish looked helplessly at her husband and he suddenly asked:

"Tippy, how would you like to go to Switzerland to school?"

"Switzer . . . Well, gracious patience!" Tippy slid out to the very edge of the cushion and stared. "I wouldn't like it at all," she said, after a thoughtful, frightened moment. "Do I have to?"

"No, Tip, of course you don't. We only thought. . . ."

"But you brought me over here so I could be with you," she reminded. "You said you had to have at least *one* child with you. My soul, if I have to go away to school, I might as well have stayed with Penny. I'd have been with *someone,* then."

There was a tight white ring around her mouth and her clasped fingers were so tightly locked that Colonel Parrish left his chair and sat down beside her. "Listen, honey," he said, laying his strong brown hand over both of hers, "I was just so eager to have you here that I didn't investigate the school situation properly. You won't have to go to Switzerland if you don't want to, because we have two other alternatives."

"What?"

"Well, one is that you go up to Munich like Arnold Macklin and the Welch boy do. There's a big high school group up there and Colonel and Mrs. Palmer said they'd be glad to have you stay with them and go to school with their kids. And you could come home for week-ends."

Tippy's tense shoulders slumped and she sat with her head bent, looking down at her father's hand on her knee. The very curve of her body was a line of dejection, and he asked, "Wouldn't you like that, honey?"

"No."

That was all she said, so he prompted, "The kids have fun. They have their dances and parties, and you could be excused early enough every Friday afternoon to come home on the train. You might have fun."

"Not in Munich." The words were wrung from Tippy and she waited a long time before she could gather more. "I'd die in Munich," she said. "I couldn't live with just ruined houses to look at and poor people. I couldn't be happy."

"Well, dear, we're doing everything we can for the people. They lost a war, Tippy, a war which they began; but we're trying to straighten them out and help them."

"I know it." It was no use telling her father that little children hadn't lost a war, or the German girls who wanted to go to dances, or Jochen who had hoped to be a doctor. He knew those things. Because of them he had brought five inexperienced young people into his home. So she only asked, "What's the other alternative?"

"That you have lessons here at home. Mrs. Tremaine will teach you. She's an officer's wife, a Vassar graduate, and has taught in a high school. She said she'd coach you and have you ready to take each term's final examinations. The Munich school will give them to you and you can get your diploma.

I haven't been entirely lax, Tippy," he said. "I did investigate all the angles."

"I know you did, Dad." Tippy withdrew one hand and stroked his gently. School had always played an important part in her life. Not because she was an excellent student, though she had managed to cling to a place in the upper half of her class, but because she had loved the fun of being with her friends and was afraid to miss a day lest something exciting happen. Education without a social reward was merely medicine without a piece of candy afterward, and she went on stroking her father's hand while she wondered if she could swallow the bitter pill.

"Look, darling," her mother proposed, sitting on the divan, too, and thinking that poor little Tippy looked like a small pet kitten crouched between two bull dogs and afraid to run. "It wouldn't take all day to do your work. You could be all through by early afternoon and then your time would be all yours."

To do what? Tippy wondered. To sit and look at the Zugspitze or take an afternoon nap? It was a jolly prospect, but she said as best she could, "It will be all right, I guess. When do I start?"

"Mrs. Tremaine said she could come on Monday, and since you brought all your books in the hold baggage, we can use those until we have the right ones sent down from Munich." Mrs. Parrish looked anxiously at her husband, even sent him a pleading lift of her eyebrows, and he offered gallantly:

"Being as how it's a Wednesday, I thought we might take in the Casa Carioca tonight. It has a marvelous ice show and I want you to see the way the floor rolls back."

Ah, thought Tippy, family night. Wednesday night, to quote Kay, was always family night, when people showed the amazing place to their children. Look, darling, see the way the floor disappears? Now where do you suppose it goes? And look at all the people. See the other little girls with their parents? Now, sit up and behave as nicely as they're doing. But she heard herself saying aloud, "That would be nice."

Her voice was automatic and polite, and it didn't deceive the two on either side of her. "All right, that's what we'll do, then," Colonel Parrish said with a sigh. "Gosh, I'm sorry about this, Tip. If I'd known how things would be, believe me, I'd never have brought you over here."

"I don't mind, Dad." Tippy relaxed against him and slid her hand back under his. "Things just take getting used to, I guess," she said, swallowing a lump in her throat and wishing she could tell him it wasn't loneliness she minded; it was being such a little person in the midst of a misery larger than hers. One more miserable person in a miserable country. And she did say enigmatically, "Maybe I can find some helpful things to do."

"That's my girl." Colonel Parrish gave her a quick kiss as Jochen pounded up the basement stairs and made it clear, with dramatic gestures, that something had gone wrong below and the roast of beef was *"kaput."*

Fumes and smoke accompanied him, and it was with great relief that the consulting three jumped up to comfort a weeping cook.

CHAPTER VII

TIPPY passed two of the longest weeks she had ever faced. Mrs. Tremaine arrived on the stroke of ten each morning and was so soft-voiced and clear in her teaching that the little sun-room was almost as silent as a public library. She and Tippy sat on a banquette built around the outer two sides of it, and faced the open door to the terrace. Their books were on a square table that filled the room; potted flowers sat on a marble window ledge just above their shoulders, and over and through the flowers they could see the mountains. Often, for long minutes at a time, the only sound to be heard was the steady drip-drip-drip of a little wall fountain where water plopped out of a bronze lion's mouth into a small copper watering can. When Tippy's head was bent in study, Mrs. Tremaine would put on her coat and slip out to sit in one of Bobby's canvas chairs on the terrace, with a book on psychology. Her sleek hair was prematurely gray and done in a bun, and she was so engrossed in her own study that Tippy often looked up to wonder how she could enjoy a life like this.

From ten o'clock until two. Five days a week, from ten o'clock until two. And then what? No doubt Mrs. Tremaine had a pleasant life to return to, Tippy decided. She could sit and read her book or think about her husband coming home and what they had planned for the evening. When she tootled off on her bicycle she knew she was going somewhere. She didn't have to stay behind to gather up books and papers, to put them in a neat pile on the window ledge and cover the table with its bright print cloth for tomorrow's breakfast, and then sit down again.

Of course, there had been the night at the Casa. That, while definitely a family night, had been fun. No one could imagine a night club as large as the Casa. It filled a building as big as a gymnasium. And when the Parrishes had climbed an inside stairway and opened a door, Tippy had gasped in pleased surprise. Far below was an oblong dance floor that might once have been a basketball court. Three tiers of floors instead of bleachers went up from three sides of it, and on each tier were tables and chairs for dining. Far away on the end wall was a Spanish balcony where a large and lusty orchestra played. Below it was a giant arch hung with red velvet curtains, and Tippy instinctively knew that behind it were the skaters' dressing rooms. The roof was high and hidden by a ceiling of airplane silk. On warm summer nights a secret mechanism could open it to a view of stars and mountains, just as chains could roll away the floor above an ice rink. The vast room was almost breath-taking in its magnitude. Family night or no family night, Tippy was glad she was there to see it.

Colonel Parrish bought a book of tickets from a girl at a desk and as her mother followed the head waiter to what, as he assured them, was the best table on the second tier, he whispered to Tippy, "This is a V.I.P. table."

"What does that mean?" she asked over her shoulder, trying to see everything at once.

"Reserved for Very Important Persons. You'll hear it a lot in Germany instead of rank."

"And what are the tickets for?"

"Food and drink. Four or five hamburgers for you, and a soft drink."

And not to let him down, Tippy had eaten heartily. There had been little else to do until the floor had disappeared and the lights dimmed. Then she became entranced with the girls and boys who skated from between the velvet curtains, with glittering costumes and swirling figures gliding over the ice to music. "Oh, it's really beautiful," she breathed, watching a girl in a diaphanous green dress waltz with a boy to the soft strains of the Blue Danube. "I've never, in all my life, seen anything lovelier than this waltz is."

"They're the stars of the show," her father answered.

Tippy leaned forward on her elbows. The girl's brown hair hung softly about her shoulders and her brown eyes smiled with her lips. She looked so free and happy, dipping and swirling with her blond partner in correct tails, as light as air. Neither she nor the boy seemed weighted with skates, for they floated over the ice or leaped apart to meet again, and once, when they were gliding around the outside of the rink, Tippy was sure the girl looked up at her table and really smiled.

And after that, the Parrishes left.

"There isn't another show, Tip," Colonel Parrish said regretfully, "and nothing more to see, unless you want to stay and dance with me."

But Tippy shook her head. "Thanks, Dad, it's a treat, but I'll skip it. I'd rather go home and think about the ice show," she answered. "I wish I could skate like the one who did the waltz. Do you think I could, if I tried?"

"You might. Why don't you write Penny to send you some skates?" he suggested, glad something had brought light to her eyes.

"I think I will."

So Tippy had dashed off her letter and now there was nothing to do but wait.

"I'm good at that," she muttered, flapping her lunch cloth back into place and setting a bowl of asters in the exact center of it.

The snow-capped peaks were dazzling in the bright fall sunshine and she thought of tramping up a low hill behind her house or even of making another attempt to return Kay's call. Kay had been out on her two other visits, when she was dressed in her best and mincing along on her highest, most uncomfortable heels. Kay was usually out, so it seemed hardly worth the effort, and she gave the flower bowl a little push that set it crooked on the cloth and made her feel better.

"Boy, what a life," she muttered, wandering through the first living room, through the second and into the third. "I'm going to bust pretty soon."

Her mother was sitting before a desk, one of the overpowering mahogany pieces, and without looking around, she said brightly, "Oh, hello. Is that you?"

"Isn't it always me?" Tippy chose a chair and sat down on her spine, her long legs in slacks straight out before her. "I should think you'd be as tired of me as I am."

"I never am, my pet. But look," Mrs. Parrish laid down her pen and swung around, "Dad telephoned that he ran into Ken in Munich this morning and invited him down for the week-end. How does that strike you?"

"Great happy day! *Grr-reat happy day!*" Tippy jumped out of her chair and gave a whoop. "Is he coming?" she broke off to ask.

"He said he'd love to. He went back to Bremerhaven to get his car and just came home. He said he'd be here tomorrow afternoon about four and for you to be ready to step."

"Step where?" Tippy sat down again to consider. The Casa, huh?" she asked, and her mother nodded. "And perhaps a cable car trip up the Kreuzeck on Sunday afternoon, with dinner at the restaurant on top. Huh?" Another nod satisfied her and she sat with her hands hanging between her knees while she considered how much else they could squeeze in. But her mother's voice brought her head up.

"Don't think, honey, that we haven't pitied you," Mrs. Parrish said. "We know it isn't right for a girl to be as lonely as you are, so we've tried to fix it. We. . . ." She reached around for her letter and said with it in her hand, "We decided to have Bobby fly over for Christmas. I just wrote him the check."

"Ye gods!" Tippy's head jerked as high as a pony's held with a check rein. "Do you mean to say," she asked, astonishment all over her face, "that you're going to spend all that money, just to bring Bobby over here so I can fight with him?"

Mrs. Parrish laughed. "Exactly," she answered. "A good fight is just what you need to make you appreciate the peace you have."

"Well, honestly." Tippy had been busy making plans for Ken's visit and, with care, could stretch her pleasant thoughts over the rest of today and tomorrow. Now Bobby was thrown in for good measure. Bobby tipped the scales with a crash and she said, frowning, "Why didn't you wait at least a week to tell me? Gosh, I've gone along for two weeks with *nothing*. Why didn't you string it out a little? You know, feed me a little today, and a little more next month, and then maybe a little more some other time? You can't give a starving person one whale of a meal, all at once."

"You poor little cat fish." Mrs. Parrish jumped up and caught Tippy's face between her two hands. "I guess I should have kept it a while," she said, bending to kiss her, "at least until I'm sure he can be away from college long enough to make the trip. But just thinking of seeing him excites me so I get in a twitchet. Won't it be wonderful, Tip?"

"It will be—something." Tippy grinned and pulled her mother down on the wide upholstered arm of her chair. "I'll be glad to see the old geezer," she said with affection, no matter how unflattering her term of address. "I even yearn for him, now and then. But tell me something. Do you think I'm kind of young for the Casa on a Saturday night?"

"Ummmm—no." Mrs. Parrish considered the matter and shook her head. "Things are different over here than they are at home," she said. "At home, you wouldn't want to go to the officers' dances at the club, but over here. . . ."

"I positively breathe dreamy sighs at the thought of it. Oh, brother!"

The next afternoon she was closer to the window than a Red Cross sticker. And when Ken's car turned in the driveway with a fine spurt of gravel, she was down the stairs before his motor was off. Even Jochen was left trailing as she cleared the side steps, her upraised arms flinging more signals than even the Scouts could think up. Her white wool dress rippled out like a fluted petunia and she came so fast and seemed so utterly brakeless that Ken jumped out and offered himself as a barrier.

"Whoa!" he said, catching her and spinning her around. "Does pretty little me cause this mad welcome?"

"You're young. You're *young!*" she cried, pushing back and staring at him. "At least you're the youngest thing I've seen, next to Jochen," she corrected. "And what a *car!*" At that her hands clasped together under her chin and Ken took a declamatory stance.

"The works," he said, sweeping out his arm in a gesture that invited her to take a good look at this rich elegance on wheels and to miss nothing. "Radio, heater, an automatic top which obeys my slightest command and finger on a button, real leather, real glass, real tin—and I might point out," he finished with sudden sadness, "it's mostly tin and not worth the fifteen hundred dollars I paid for it, and haven't earned, yet. But it's pretty, isn't it?"

"It certainly becomes you." Tippy admired the sleek, black car again and tucked her arm through his. "That's Jochen standing on the steps," she whispered. "You must say *Grüss Gott* to him when I introduce him. It's a Bavarian custom."

"Right."

Ken grinned at Jochen and pumped his hand in a genuine

way. He also slipped part of a package of cigarettes into Jochen's pocket when he went to bring in a heavy canvas bag, and when Tippy looked sad he said cheerfully, "Makes me think of the way I rustled in a fraternity house. I had to prep somewhere for my West Point exams and Dad couldn't afford it. He was a small country minister with five kids, so I got a job at the State U. Boy, I fired enough furnaces and carried enough trays to warm and feed myself for a year. And look at me, now. Strong, stalwart, healthy. . . ." He puffed out his chest and Tippy gave him a light tap that set him coughing.

"You dope," she said, laughing as she had feared she never would laugh again. "Come and *grüssen* the parents."

It was such a gay foursome around the dinner table that evening. Jochen tripped constantly over the rug, apologized so profusely and shouted so audibly down his dumb waiter in the pantry, that he would have provided enough whispered amusement had there been nothing else to laugh about. And it was over coffee cups in the living room that Ken said:

"I hope you won't worry if I keep your daughter out on the late side tonight. I've made a few plans and it may be in the small hours of morning before I return her to you."

"Well, that depends on the plans." Colonel Parrish looked no more perturbed than if Ken had said he was going to church, and Tippy put down her cup and gave undivided attention to her immediate future.

"Well, sir, I'm not without friends in Garmisch," Ken explained, elevating one of his crooked eyebrows and looking pleased with himself. "At least, I know one couple, and I'd like Tip to know them, too. The young Vanderhoefs. Van was a great guy at the Point. He came along with the batch that was graduated just as war broke and shot up to be a lieutenant colonel. And he's held the rank. Jeannie's an army girl and . . . well, she's pretty special. I used to know her when I visited my uncle and aunt and I tagged her the way I did Penny at Fort Arden. And then I ran into them, later, when they were up at West Point. I gave them a ring when I knew I was coming down here today and they asked us to sit at their table at the Casa and to go home with them afterward. I think they're just the folks for Tippy to know."

"I think so, myself." Colonel Parrish nodded and settled the matter by saying, "I've met them and they're nice youngsters. Take Tippy along and have a good time."

It all went so smoothly that Tippy wondered if it hadn't been rehearsed in her absence. "Do something about poor Tip," her father probably had said in Munich, and Ken had done it. Even her mother looked too arch and eager, as if a backward bird were about to hop out of the nest, and Tippy looked from one to the other then burst out laughing. "You don't fool me a bit," she said. "Not one teeny smidgen bit. I know you were sunk when I didn't like Kay Macklin, and it drives you crazy to see me going around looking so glum all the time. But, just the same I think you're darlings." She jumped up and ruffled her father's hair, gave her mother a peck on her cheek, and stopped with a swish on the other side of the coffee table. "What if I don't like the Vanderhoefs either?" she said with her head on one side. "I've grown kind of peculiar, you know."

"You'll like them," Ken promised. "Now go and put on a new mouth."

"Do I wear this dress?"

"The same. You'll tear their hearts out in something new from New York. White wool with gold embroidery? Sister, you'll stop the show."

"And my flat gold sandals. If I can't get around in those. . . ." Tippy ran out the door and down the hall.

It was the first time her feet had ever patted the long hall carpet so lightly and with such swift grace, and she was back

[93]

before the others had finished their coffee. "Well, let's go!" she cried, holding out a short fur jacket. "You started this thing but I'm going to finish it. It's time, isn't it?"

"Just exactly the right time." Ken looked at her standing before him. Her tan curls were brushed back from her eager face and her eyes were filled with flecks of gold like the embroidered yoke on her dress. She was a fairy thing, and he set his cup in its saucer with a clink that would have shattered a cheaper piece of china. "Let's go," he said, and got up quickly.

Jochen was at the door to speed their departure, and the maids a giggling group at the head of the basement stairs. Tippy wondered how the news had spread so quickly and for one moment the gold in her eyes tarnished and her dimples dimmed. Then she opened her jacket to show them her dress and summoned all the German words she knew to tell them that sometime . . . soon . . . perhaps . . . they could go where she was going.

"As if they could," she said to Ken in the car. "Poor things."

But he only grinned and shifted his gear to reverse. "You haven't met Jeannie, yet," he answered. "Jeannie of the light brown hair."

"What has Jeannie got to do with it?"

"Just wait and see." And with that she had to be content.

The Casa Carioca on Saturday night was a different place from the same club, on a Wednesday. It had more glitter. Tables were crowded, the orchestra played with a dash, waiters hurried. Tippy looked at the crowd on the dance floor and walked eagerly beside Ken as they made their way along one side and almost across the far end.

"Oh, there they are," he said, looking down at a table for four in the exact center of the lowest tier.

"Where?"

[94]

"Right above the wall around the rink. Come on."

He led the way to a wide flight of wooden steps, and going down beside him, Tippy wondered just how the Vanderhoefs would look. She was quite unprepared for an officer who, in spite of his advanced rank, seemed as young as Ken, who was just as tall, and was also equipped with a double cowlick. Young Colonel Vanderhoef's hair would have curled had he let it, and the cowlick made an obliging swirl. He had a slender face that was almost square at the chin, and deep-set blue eyes. All this was flashed to Tippy while he got up to greet them, then she looked down at his wife.

"This is Jeanne Ann," Ken said. "But everyone calls her Jeannie."

Jeanne Ann's hair was darker than the light brown Ken had given her, and as she reached up with a smile, Tippy saw little but her great gray-green eyes. Under arched dark brows, the eyes dominated her whole face. They had little flecks of brown in them, and Tippy thought, they *are* her face. It was some time before she had a chance to look at Jeanne Ann's profile, to see the way her hair swept back from her broad smooth forehead and how perfect her straight nose was, or her round chin, below a mouth that was generous and beautifully shaped.

She wore a hand-painted blouse tucked into a full black skirt and held by a gold belt. And she rattled on much the way Penny did, pointing out special friends of hers, while her husband caught up on the past with Ken. Then the orchestra shifted to a Strauss waltz, and as if at a signal, the young Vanderhoefs pushed back their chairs.

"Our dance, Jeannie," Van said, explaining with a happy grin, "The band always waits till we get our wind up, then plays this for us."

And when she saw them on the floor together, Tippy understood why. They were perfect in their way, just as the girl

[95]

and boy on skates were; and it was almost with reluctance that she took Ken's outstretched hand and let her own chair slide back.

"Having fun?" he asked, when they were caught in the crowd, and she nodded.

"The best time I've had in Garmisch—or anywhere else," she added honestly. "Oh, my soul, there's Kay."

Kay Macklin had shifted her personality for the evening to that of a South Sea beauty and wore an off-the-shoulder batiste blouse and a red skirt as tightly wrapped as a sarong. An artificial flower bloomed above each ear, and Tippy stared at her cloud of hair. "My goodness," she said, "it looked short a couple of weeks ago, I swear it did."

Then Kay saw her, also saw the presentable young man she was with, and not only returned the stare but flashed a smile with it. "Where are you sitting?" she called.

"Up at the end." Tippy released one finger of the hand Ken held and pointed, but Kay scowled and looked away.

"*Now,* what did I say that was wrong?" she whispered. "Surely *that* couldn't have made her mad."

"We're up with the V.I.P. bunch," he answered. "Not that my rank gets me there, you understand, but the Vanderhoefs are regulars. They come on Wednesday nights and bring the servants, one by one, and on Saturday nights they. . . ."

"What do you mean, they bring the servants?" Tippy looked up to ask. "Could I do it, too?"

But the lights had dimmed. The music stopped and he guided her up the short flight of steps to the first tier.

"Here, Tippy," Jeanne Ann said with a rush, as they came up, "you take the chair at this end of the table and, Ken, you take the one at the other end. Van and I've seen the show a hundred times, but this is a new one tonight and I want you to be right by the rail where you can watch. And it gets cold down here so close to the ice, so put on your coat." She slid into her own fox jacket while she directed things, then stood looking up. "Oh, there goes Inge!" she cried, waving to a girl who was walking around a narrow runway, high above them. "A square in that silk sky will open and she'll come down, sitting in a silver moon."

Tippy looked up, too, and recognized the dark girl who had skated to the Strauss waltz. "Do you know her?" she asked eagerly, as the dance floor rolled away beneath her chair.

"Umhum. She and Robert will come and sit with us after the show. Van," she sat down and asked, "have you ordered their hamburgers?"

"I have. Three apiece, with catsup." He, too, sat down beside his wife and he winked at Tippy. "You'd think she was responsible for this show," he said with an easy grin. "She's worried more over Inge in that silly moon!"

"Sh." Jeanne Ann leaned toward him and made a little face which he returned. Then as the orchestra began a lively air and the velvet curtains parted for a spangled chorus to glide through, his shoulder moved nearer to hers and their heads stayed close together while they made whispered comments.

At the end of each number they applauded vigorously and Tippy enjoyed them as much as she did the intricate dances before her. And when the show had ended and the wooden floor had rumbled out again, Jeanne Ann thumped the table with her fist and wailed, "It is, it is, Van, isn't it?"

"Well, could be." Van's engaging grin spread and he said in a loud aside behind his hand, "Miss Fix-it, doesn't like Inge's dress in the Spanish number. She's been predicting that it's too skimpy, that it would look like an umbrella when it blew out. And it did. I'm not a critical character, myself, but I'll have to admit it did. Oh-oh. *Now* we'll hear all about it."

The two stars were coming along the aisle, the dark girl who had a somber face, now that she wore no make-up and wasn't smiling, and who wore a brown suit with a white blouse instead of her disputed costume of the last act; the very blond boy in a tweed jacket and gray slacks. Now and then they stopped for a few words at other tables, but after an exchange of sentences they always pushed on.

"Oh, Inge!" Jeanne Ann cried excitedly, whirling around on her chair and knocking over one of the two extra ones a waiter had squeezed in, "It was simply *gorgeous!* It was wonderful—but the dress *isn't* right and they'll have to put the waltz number back in. The whole show simply falls flat without that waltz number."

"I like to do it best of all. Robert does, too, but. . . ."

The amused skater broke off with a shrug and Tippy was so surprised at her perfect English that she almost forgot to listen to Jeanne Ann Vanderhoef's haphazard introductions. She thought she heard Inge Wolfsteiner and Robert Unger, but wasn't sure and was too interested in the pair to address them, anyway. Inge had taken the righted chair and her face was bright and alive again. She chattered rapidly of all the things that had gone wrong in the show, leaned forward to look at her partner and ask, "Did you notice that, Robert?" and finally saw her plate and said, "Oh, thank you, Van. I am so hungry."

And sometimes the conversation went off into German. Jeanne Ann could swing from one language to the other and when Robert's good-looking florid face became blank, either she or Inge would put him on the path again. He sat squeezed in at the corner beside Tippy, and once he turned to her and asked, more hesitant and carefully than Inge would have to do, "Does our skating talk bore you?"

"Oh, no," she answered, shaking her head and afraid she might wake up to find herself dreaming. "I love it."

"You skate, too?"

"A little."

"Then you must come down to the Casa with Jeannie

some morning. She skates after our practise is over. When the ice is—is. . . ."

"Chopped to bits," Inge helped him out, laughing. "Poor Jeannie, she is always sitting down."

"And Tippy can sit with me." Jeanne Ann laughed, too, but she rubbed the back of her silk skirt tenderly. "One of the girls will lend you an old pair of skates if you haven't any," she said. Then she pushed back her chair. "Shall we go home?" she asked.

"Leave us be on our way." Van tossed his empty book of tickets on the table beside Ken's and spread out his cigarette tip. "Kick in there, Prescott," he said amiably. "The Vanderhoef reserve is low this month."

"Will do." Ken laid six white cylinders in the line and went around to hold Tippy's coat. "What do you think of them?" he whispered over her shoulder as her arms groped for her sleeves.

"I think they're all darling," she answered, going up the steps and along the aisle beside him. "And if this is what Kay meant by having Germans crowd in at your table, I'd like to take a bigger table next time."

It surprised her to hear herself speak of coming to the Casa again, not because it seemed improbable that she would be invited to come, but because she was so certain she would sit right at that same delightful table; and she listened to Ken say:

"Van has to be away a lot and Inge stays with Jeannie for weeks at a time. How old do you think she is?"

"Inge? I don't know." She hesitated while she tried to decide. Jeanne Ann had mentioned during the evening that she and Van had three children at home, and Ken had said Van came out of the Point in '40. Inge was their friend and often looked older than Jeannie when she was gravely listening, so perhaps. . . .

"She's just eighteen," Ken told her, not to keep her guess-

[99]

ing any longer. "And Robert's twenty-two. They're war children, you know. Jeannie told me tonight that Robert's family was once as rich as they come and Inge's father wasn't poor, either. They used to skate together for fun as kids and now they're glad to have a job. One that's paid by the Americans," he added.

"Oh, dear, I know they are." Tippy saw Kay at a table on the top tier, quite close to the door. There were no German girls at her table. In fact, she and a dreary young officer were quite alone, and with a quick pull on Ken's arm, she caught up with the four in front of her. She even made a great point of putting her hand on Inge's sleeve and saying the first thing that came into her head. It turned out to be, "I do hope you're coming to Jeannie's with us," then she turned and sent a naughty, triumphant wave down to Kay.

CHAPTER VIII

TIPPY thought she had never seen anything quite like the Vanderhoef house. It was in beautiful order when they went into it, and was complete with a set of living rooms coupled together, with overpowering antiques and paintings; but in half an hour it was a shambles. Army couples drifted in. An aluminum coffee pot sat on a table beside a silver coffee urn, rugs were rolled back and people danced to the music of an accordion and two violins.

"Louis' Hungry Three," Van had introduced the trio when he brought it in, while a short dark man, a cadaverous tall one, and a little fellow who bounced on the balls of his feet, tried not to look as hungry as their name implied. "They're through at the Post Hotel for the night, so feed 'em, somebody."

Jeanne Ann was down on her knees before the coffee table, slicing ham and putting it between bread. She was quite accustomed to this threesome turning up, since lights in the Vanderhoef house acted like a dove cote to homing pigeons. Van had given the musicians their title and they always did their very best to live up to it before they offered their music in payment, and she slid around to hold up the sandwich plate.

At intervals a curly black puppy and a tiger cat romped through, intent on a game of their own, and later a small girl sat on the sofa. A very small girl, only two years old and wrapped in a pink blanket. Van had brought her in, too, but sitting in the crook of his arm. Her round face was flushed with sleep, her brown hair stood up like a whisk broom and she smiled a wide pearly smile. "Hey, Jeannie," he called above the racket, ruffling up his own hair in a comical effort to cope with this strange situation. "Lee says we woke her up. She says she can't go back to sleep, so what do we do?"

"Put her down, she'll be tired soon." Jeanne Ann winked at the baby and gave her a cookie, then went back to her work. So there sat the small Lee beside Inge, who watched over her with tender eyes.

Dancing with Ken, Tippy never knew exactly when the baby disappeared, for Louis' Hungry Three had finished most of the ham and were sending out a medley of German songs. She moved blissfully to the soft strains of *You Are My Heart Alone* and Ken smiled down at her. "Do you see any dragon around here?" he asked in a soft teasing voice, hoping this was the time to banish her fears forever. And she had to shake her head.

"No," she said, looking thoughtful. "Jeannie makes me think such a lot of Penny. I wonder if she'll let me tag along the way they used to let you? And I'd—I'd like to know Inge, too."

"I think you will. They like you."

"They do? Are you sure?"

"They think you're a darling." He swept her off and contented himself with looking down at the top of her head that stayed just below his chin, no matter what steps he tried.

Tippy knew it was late, very late. Later, in fact, than she had ever stayed out. But she had permission to be here, so clung desperately to every minute of it. She danced with several officers who were kind to her and she talked with their young wives about all the latest styles in America. And then, just when Ken was holding her jacket and the evening had to end, Louis took his violin down from his sagging chin and said in a quaint mixture of English and German:

"We come—*und* do two t'ings. *Nein*, tree. We eat." He stopped and waited for hearty applause to answer his sentence and patted his flat stomach with his bow. "We play Goo-ood Moosik," he said, rolling his black eyes appreciatively before going on. "We play, you dance. *Ist auch*—alzo goo-ood. But now. *Ach,* now, comes de tree t'ing. We play de *Vienner Blut. Und Frau* Vanderhoef—*und Herr Oberst* Van-derhoef—dey dance."

Louder applause greeted the end of his speech and Tippy sat right down where she was in the middle of the hall arch-way, to watch.

"Oh my, oh me, we can't." Jeanne Ann protested. But as the clapping of hands went on, she changed her mind and pushed out of the group around Louis. "All right," she said. "There's nothing I'd rather do than waltz with Van, so if you can bear it, here we go. If you don't want to watch, just eat and drink. Shall we, *Herr Oberst?*"

"*Gnädige Frau.*" Van grinned and encircled her waist.

But no one thought of the plate of sandwiches or steaming percolator. They stood in little groups and watched the two blended figures; and Tippy was torn between becoming a skater like Inge, or part of a dance team.

"Oh dear," she sighed, when nothing, not even whistles and bravos could make them repeat their performance, "now I *do* have to go home. Well," she was philosophical as she said her good-bys, "at least I've had one of the most perfect evenings I've ever had. And, Jeannie, thank you, so much."

They stood in the front door and Jeanne Ann said, "We loved having you. We'll do it again, soon. And in the mean-time, please come over whenever you want to. I'm always around." Then she chuckled. "Herr Breitski will probably want to paint your portrait," she prophesied. "He's always around, too, painting us, and I've run out of subjects for him. I do hope your tires are still on your car." And she leaned out to call, "Ludolf?" A deep voice came back in a gutteral, "Ya?" and she nodded. "They're on," she said. "So many cars have lost everything but their bodies when they've been left out at a party, that we have to have a guard. Good night, Tippy. Good night, Ken."

"Good night, and thank you again." Tippy was going down the steps as wide awake as an owl.

The mountains were silvery white in the moonlight, as Ken turned the car down a hill toward the sleeping town. "Let's take a short detour," he suggested, rattling over one of the wooden bridges that spanned the swift, shallow Loisach River and driving slowly along a narrow street. "The town looks so sweet and peaceful after its gone to bed."

"And I suppose that's when your little man of the mountain comes down and walks around," she said, matching his mood. "That's probably the reason he thought the war didn't come to Garmisch. He just goes around like a night watchman; and when everything's locked up and safe, he's like Louis, he thinks it's goo-ood."

"Well, isn't it?" he looked at her quizzically and she shook her head.

"No," she answered. "You heard Jeanne Ann say that people steal the tires right off of the cars, and we were told to keep our house locked." They were passing the painted hotel and she pointed it out, then went on, "I don't think it's so safe when you can't leave your car in its own driveway." But he only countered:

"I remember that my dad had a burglar alarm for our car, during the war. He was afraid to leave it even on the main street of our town without having the alarm hooked up. There was a shortage of rubber then, and accessories, even cars; and a powerful ring dealt in stolen stuff. Well, the same thing's true over here, now. You've got a black market to tempt a hungry people. Jeannie and Van aren't fighting the black market ring, they simply hire a guard to protect their property. And remember this, Tip," he pointed out: "every German is listed with the police, and they're more scared of the American soldiers than we are of them."

"And of the dragon." She leaned back and smiled. "I'm not so scared of the dragon, now," she said.

"Do you know what he is?"

"Not yet, but I will. You keep showing me little pieces of him. About the time I'm ready to go home, I'll fit him together like a jig saw puzzle and I'll probably laugh because he'll look so silly." She turned and put both hands on the leather seat between them. "I guess I should be very grateful," she said earnestly, "that you came over on the same boat I did. What would I have done if you hadn't?"

"It's too dreadful to contemplate, so leave us turn our thoughts to brighter subjects. Have you been up to Oberammergau?"

"No." She shook her head and stayed as she was, watching him.

"Then we'll buzz up tomorrow, today," he corrected. "And we'll swing around to look at *Schloss* Linderhof that the mad king Ludwig built, and the Ettal Monastery. My goodness, child," he said, "you aren't getting any education at all. I'll bet you didn't even know Richard Strauss lived here in Garmisch."

"I didn't." Tippy leaned back now and laughed. She had quite finished with her serious thinking. Ken had swept away her doubts as he always did, and she said placidly, "The only trouble is, I had planned to entertain you and have all the ideas. I had thought we'd go up the Kreuzeck."

"We'll go up there this winter when we can ski." The bridge rattled under their tires again and the car picked its way up a road full of holes. "Don't let me sleep too late," Ken urged, when the Parrish house loomed up like a bright, lighted beacon against the mountains. "I don't want to waste my holiday sleeping."

"We'll make every minute of it count," she promised, as eager as he was for nature to fill a rush order on her system's restoration.

[105]

And Sunday went by on wings. It flew so fast that it swept Ken off with it and left her to turn off the downstairs lights in a sleepy daze.

"It was such fun," she told her mother the next afternoon, after she had set the little bowl of flowers in the center of the lunch cloth and had lovingly rearranged them so that each blossom received its share of sunlight. "Ken kept pretending we lived in Ludwig's beautiful palace and we were always getting left behind the rest of the tourists and didn't hear half the guide said. And when we got in the artificial cave, he. . . ." Tippy broke off and asked, "Did you know Ludwig had a cave built right inside of a mountain?" And at her mother's headshake, she said, "Well, he did. It's an enormous thing; and wherever he wanted a rock, he built a rock. And a lake, with an island in it. He built the whole business so an opera company could come and sing Lohengrin, with Wagner directing it. He was going to sit up on a cliff, something else he had built, to listen to it, but the company wouldn't sing for a one-man audience so he couldn't do it. It's no wonder the government said he was crazy, and exiled him. Gosh!" She put Ludwig into the past where he belonged and asked, "What do I do, now?"

"Must you do something?"

"Well," Tippy sat down to consider the matter. "I think so," she said, nodding. "The last thing Ken said was, 'Now, Tip, keep busy.' He's sort of taken me in hand, you know," she explained frankly, "at your and Dad's request. And I can't keep busy unless I get started."

"It seems to me you've been busy all morning."

"Oh, studying, pooh. Can't you suggest something more pleasant?"

Mrs. Parrish named a list of activities that began with a browse through the Post Exchange and ended with a call on Jeanne Ann Vanderhoef. And Tippy chose the last suggestion and asked:

"Would it be all right—so soon?"

"I think it would," said her mother, amused. "It always has been considered correct to pay your respects after a social evening."

"Then I think I'll go. I know you're teasing me, you always are when you bring high-powered words into play, but I'll fool you and go." Tippy looked down at her plaid wool dress and decided, "I'll go just as I am. I don't want her to think another Kay Macklin tripped in." Mid-afternoon exultation was so unexpected that she minced through the living room, flipping imaginary ashes on the seat of a chair and looking as if she might fall apart. "How's that?" she asked at the door. "Do you like it or are you glad I'm me?"

"I'm glad."

Mrs. Parrish was glad for several reasons, and the most important one was because Tippy was going somewhere. She watched the car sweep down the driveway, waved in answer to a toot of its horn, and mentally checked off the days until Bobby would arrive to whip the turbid mass of Parrishes into a froth. "Oh, dear," she sighed to herself. "We used to be such a busy, family."

And a little later, Tippy was expressing exactly the same thought in a different assortment of words. She had rung the Vanderhoef doorbell to be greeted by a small boy in a cowboy suit. He might have been Colonel Vanderhoef returned to the age of six, uncombed and unwashed, and he opened the door enough for her to squeeze through. "Look out for the tent," he shouted. "We're crossing the plains. Do you want to see my mother?"

"I'd like to," she answered, wondering how he could hear her above the war whoops of a hand painted Indian tribe on the stairs. "If you aren't afraid the Indians will steal your property while you tell her."

"I guess they might, so you'd better do it. She's in the dining room getting her picture painted."

"Then, I'll find her." Tippy stepped around a pink down comfort stretched over two chairs and the largest hobby horse she had ever seen, and the furious game began again.

She felt timid, hesitating in the living room, for far at the end, beyond the dining room door, conversational German was going on at a great rate. She was wondering whether she should back out and start over or send the reluctant cowboy on a mission, when a chair scraped on the tiled dining room floor and Jeanne Ann appeared in the archway.

"Hi, there," she said, in pleased surprise. "You're just in time for coffee and to see my portrait." She picked up the box of cigarettes she had come for, and asked, "Didn't anyone bother to let you in?"

"A little boy opened the door and told me where you were."

"Craig." Jeanne Ann nodded and laughed. "Thomas is off today," she explained in an off-hand fashion, as if sure Tippy would understand the running of a German household, "and it's coffee time in the basement. And wouldn't you know," she added, "that as nice as it is outside the gang would choose to set up a tent in the hall? Oh, well, come meet the Breitskis."

She led Tippy to the dining room where a round little man sat on a straight chair before an easel, while a woman and pretty young girl looked over his shoulder. "Frau Breitski," Jeanne Ann said, "Herr Breitski, Marga, this is Fraulein Parrish." And they sprang to attention.

"Ah," Herr Breitski exclaimed, dipping low over Tippy's hand and jerking upright so quickly that his gray hair fell forward, then back, as if on a hinge. "*Ich habe fur Ihnen gemahlt, nicht?*" and his daughter explained shyly, in English:

"Vatie means that he painted a sign for your door when you came."

"Oh, the *welcome* sign." Tippy was happy to meet the painter of such a work of art and she told the eager three how much it had pleased her mother. "Tell them," she said, when

Marga had translated for her, "that my mother has put it in a frame and says she will always keep it. And, please, go on with your coffee."

"We have just finished," Marga answered. "We always like to come by for Vatie and have coffee and a cigarette with Mrs. Vanderhoef. Afternoon coffee," she explained with the same shy look, "is a great treat for us."

"And something you won't even bother about when you get to America," Jeanne Ann told her, giving Tippy a cup and adding, in her pleased, excited way, "Marga's engaged to a sergeant. The Breitskis don't know how they can bear it to have her marry and go so far away."

Tippy looked at the girl again. She had sweet features and a look of delicate breeding that overshadowed her short dress and worn shoes that had come loose from their soles. And she said, "Perhaps I can't leave them. After all. . . ."

"*Ya.*" Frau Breitski understood her words and nodded. "You go," she reassured her daughter, confidently. "And now we must go also. Come, Vatie."

It was hard to pry Herr Breitski loose from his painting and he was so slow washing his brushes and putting them away that he managed to smoke two more cigarettes, and it was with a sigh of relief that Jeanne Ann closed the front door behind them and returned to drop limply into a chair.

"I'm really terribly fond of them," she said, smiling apologetically at Tippy. "But Herr Breitski comes and paints, and paints and paints. He likes to be where it's warm and have a good lunch," she said tiredly. "And I've had Mrs. Wanger here, too, today. She's old and has trouble with her stomach. Oh, dear, it's time for Trudchen to leave. 'Scuse me a minute." She pulled herself to her feet again and went out to the hall. More German drifted in and when she came back she explained, "Trudchen's the sewing woman and always the last to leave. I used to drive her home, or Van did, and usually the Breitskis, too. Poor guy, he always came home to a house full

[109]

of Germans. No matter how tired he was, he always had to deliver one somewhere and listen to a yakaty-yak that must have driven him crazy. So I inaugurated the five o'clock peace. You won't recognize us at five o'clock, so stay and watch it."

She laughed and curled up in a corner of the divan, her brown head pressed against a pillow. Tippy wanted to stay, but she had to say, instead, "I can't, but I know what you mean. We used to be sort of hectic, too."

"Then stay a bit and watch us. I think it's beginning. At least I hear the tent leaving the hall."

The tent was certainly leaving. Chairs crashed into one another and overturned, and a trail of pink comfort could be seen through the archway, dragging up the stairs with the dog and cat on the end of it. "Mother would have a fit," Jeanne Ann said calmly, "if she could see one of the pair she gave me." And she laughed and added, "It isn't much worse than when I played bride in her best lace bedspread. Oh joy! The confusion is over."

The small black poodle trotted in and seated himself in a corner. "Good Rover," she praised, and he curled up contentedly. "Good Mooshie," she added, as the cat jumped up on a chair. And, amazingly soon, they were followed by Craig. His red gold hair was combed back in spikes, honest testimony that a wet comb had passed through, and a scrubbed face and neck met the round webbing of a blue-and-white striped jersey. Even his blue flannel shorts were creased and his woolen socks ended in neat cuffs on his thin little legs.

He was followed by a pretty little girl, twice as old as he and even cleaner. She had blue eyes and long yellow braids, and she went straight to Tippy and waited.

"This is Miss Parrish, Inge," Jeanne Ann said, smiling at the child as she made a prompt curtsy. And then she explained into Tippy's bewilderment, "The two Inges aren't related. They just happen to have the same name, so we say big Inge and little Inge to keep them straight. Little Inge is Craig's best friend. She comes as soon as her German school is over and goes home after supper. We couldn't get on without little Inge."

Tippy looked at the child. Her sweater and skirt were exactly what every twelve year old girl in America was wearing, and her braids ended in red butterfly bows. And seeing Tippy's look of amazement, Jeannie winked.

She waited while Craig chose a deck of cards from a drawer, and when the two were playing a quiet game of fish beside the unconscious Rover, she said in a low voice, "One day she appeared to play with Craig and we noticed that she kept coming back. At first, she just played with the children and then went home. She was such a sweet little thing that finally we brought her inside, as stray a kitten as Mooshy ever was. She's a really brilliant student, but she's missed her childhood, you see. She's a six-year-old when it comes to playing and I don't see how I'd get along without her. Craig's too big for a nurse and he's so safe when he's with Inge. So, willy-nilly," she finished, with a comical wave of her hand, "the Vanderhoefs find themselves with a fourth child, who is five years older than the length of time they've been married. And here comes the rest of my brood."

Small Lee trotted in, looking like a pink bunny in a snow suit and attached by the hand to a young nurse who carried a baby. The baby was encased in a blue zipper bag and Jeanne Ann said, "Hi, Christa," then reached up and pulled her out of her furlined cocoon. Family group," she said, holding one and helping the other climb up beside her.

"They make me homesick for ours," Tippy answered, suddenly sad. "Parri's about the age of Lee. She belongs to my sister, Penny. David has two. Little Langdon, who's a little older than Christa, and Davy. Davy. . . ." she hesitated a moment, looking at Craig who was gleefully shouting, "Fish," then went on, "Davy had polio." And quite without effort, she found herself telling about it.

[111]

She talked of them all, and especially of Penny whom Jeanne Ann had seen in a play. "I think you're a lot alike," she ended, when it was almost five o'clock and she stood up to go. "The other night, I kept feeling as if I were out with Penny. We have such fun together."

"Then stay and have dinner with us. I'll go tell the cook." Jeanne Ann jumped up with the gurgling baby hanging on her hip. But Tippy shook her head.

"I really can't," she said. "I want to, goodness knows, because you even carry Christa the way Penny does Parri, all lopsided and hanging, but I think I ought to go home and make a five o'clock hour for Dad. He's sort of like what you said about Van, except—poor Dad, he hasn't much to come home to any more, just Mums and me. Perhaps I can make it a little gayer. Oh, golly, Jeannie, thanks."

Without understanding why, she reached out in a quick hug, and it was the same spontaneous kind she always gave Penny.

CHAPTER IX

So Tippy had the Vanderhoefs and set out to copy them. Not by bringing assorted sizes of children into the house, for she doubted if her father would have enjoyed that; but she did decide to buy a dog and find a cat to go with it.

"He's got to be a Rover," she told herself when she started her search. But the town was out of miniature French poodles. It had an extra doberman and two dachshunds, but no Rovers. And a stray kitten was no more to be found than a fine new automobile.

"Imagine a town without little cats," she said to her mother, after a fruitless day of looking. "Of course, I know the Germans can't afford to feed them, so I suppose they drown them all, and I've even heard they eat them, but you'd think I'd find at least one walking around." And Ken did no better in Munich.

"No poodles," he reported over the telephone. "Could you use a nice police pup with a pedigree about a mile long?"

But Tippy had set her heart on a French poodle and a cat. The only police dog she remembered was a German Shepherd named Woofy. The Parrishes had owned him long ago, and he had been given away because he had made short work of anything smaller than he was. She wanted something that would cavort through the house in the daytime and sit at attention when five o'clock came. She wanted something small that she could cuddle and love. So she let the owner keep his pedigreed pup and went on searching.

But she did turn herself into a lively young welcome for her father's return. Days flew by while she sat for her portrait and pushed the amiable Breitskis out at a quarter to five. Wednesday nights became servants' night at the Casa instead of just family night, as one by one she added her little flock to the Vanderhoefs' and watched their eyes grown round and bright with wonder. And Ken would come down, now and then, for week-ends.

The Autumn air had grown crisp and cold when he brought her a new pair of skis. Snow had crept farther down the mountains and had added white capes to the caps they had worn so long, and Tippy's breath came out in smokey puffs when she posed on the lawn for a picture.

"Oh, golly, I'm awkward," she fussed, trying to manage her poles and hold the pose he wanted. "If I can't walk around on grass what will I ever do in the snow?" Her plaid scarf blew out in the wind and cold air whistled up the sleeves of her bright blue ski suit. "And I'll freeze to death in this outfit. It felt fine when I tried it on in the store," she said with a shiver, straightening up and not noticing that Ken had clicked his camera. "But even if I put a sweater underneath, how will I keep warm?"

"By not trying to be so stylish. By wearing a soldier's jacket with a fur-lined parka," he answered, amused because his picture had caught Tippy with her mouth open and one foot in the air. "Now get set and we'll try it again. Practise bending your knees a little."

So Tippy resumed her pose, and for the next few weeks spent a great deal of time gliding up and down the living rooms in a crouching position. And at last a light snow sifted down on the low hills behind her house. It was a slushy, soft snow, but she put on the fleece-lined, canvas coat her father had drawn from the quartermaster and shouldered her skis. And she spent several hours falling down the hill and getting up, or just sitting with her skis crossed like a railroad sign while she wondered what to do next.

But at last she could sail down the hill. She could do it as well as Craig who swooped like a small brown pixie in front of her, and began to look for higher slopes to conquer.

And November slid away and the Post Exchange was filled with imported gifts for Christmas. She found a musical powder box for Alice and wasted several days deciding on something for Peter. In spite of having his photograph on her dressing table, he seemed very far away and dim; and she couldn't remember what his likes and dislikes were, what he could use or what he couldn't.

"You'd better hurry, honey," her mother warned, with each day's passing. "It's much too late for the mails, and it's only by luck and good fortune that the Petersons are sailing and are kind enough to take the package. I sent Penny's and David's boxes ages ago."

"Yep, I know you did." Tippy sighed and tried to concentrate on Peter.

"His eyes are gray," she remembered, "and straight. They don't droop down like Kens. And his hair is short and behaves itself. He likes. . . ." What did he like? Not old lady Zugspite or pretending he was crazy King Ludwig, or dropping into the Post Hotel where all the overland stages used to stop, and sitting in the old taproom while Louis' Hungry Three played opera for him. No, Peter might not like these things. She must look for something gay and amusing. So she found a rare old stein that was made like the face of a merry old man, and after she had wrapped it in red tissue paper, wrote a card that said, "Ken. From the little old man of the mountain." And she sent three tennis balls to Peter.

She knew it was an unimaginative gift, especially when a package arrived from him that was heavy and carefully wrapped, but it was the best she could do. She had too many other people on her mind.

The maids had to have sweaters, new length skirts, and a pink, silk nightgown apiece. And after Christmas, Jochen could go safely out in new serge trousers that had a whole

[115]

seat and could sleep in red-and-white striped pajamas. She haunted the Post Exchange. She was there when it opened its doors and made dozens of trips up and down its steep stairs, to different departments.

"We're going to have a whale of a Christmas," she said one evening, when she was sitting on the living room floor, surrounded by tissue paper and boxes. "I got a tree picked out. It's up on the hill and always gets in my way when I'm skiing. When Bobby comes, we'll go up and cut it. Did we bring our box of Christmas ornaments?"

"Honey," her father lowered his paper and looked down at her, "we've been thinking of taking a trip to Switzerland for Christmas. Just milling it over, you know. How would you like it?"

Tippy dropped her scissors and stared back at him. "Do you mean, not be home on Christmas?" she cried. "Why, I never heard of people staying in a hotel on Christmas!"

"We thought Bobby might enjoy it," Mrs. Parrish explained in a rush. "He won't have very long over here you know, and he should see something more than Garmisch. Dad heard of a wonderful ski resort and wrote to ask if we could make reservations. It isn't a very long drive from here."

"Well, I never!" Tippy began to wish Bobby would stay in America. She dropped her eyes to the paper she had been cutting and said while she puckered it into folds, "I told the girls about all the things we would do, Hilde and Annie and Bertha and Maria. About the tree and having a turkey. And we decided to sing carols on Christmas Eve the way the Germans do. Annie has been practising them so she can play for us."

"Yes, I've heard her." Mrs. Parrish's tone was dry as she remembered the cotton she had stuffed in her ears when Tippy was giving music lessons. "But Jochen will be with his family, and Annie and Bertha want to spend the day with their sister.

Hilde said her *fiancé* has invited her to visit his parents in Chiemsee, and. . . ."

"Oh, dear, you've fixed it all up. I suppose you fixed Maria up, too?"

"Well, after all, isn't it right, honey?" Colonel Parrish laid his copy of the *Stars and Stripes* over his knee and took off his reading glasses. "They're Germans, Tippy," he reminded, "and they'd rather spend their holiday with their own people. They'll even get a vacation."

"But what about . . .?" Tippy almost asked, "about Ken?" but bit her lips and sat looking down. Ken had been invited for Christmas. He had been invited and now he would be uninvited. "Sorry," her father would say. "We won't be home." She looked at the paper until she knew every flaw in the texture of it, where it was a bright pure red and where it had dark streaks and black spots of dye. Then she jerked up her head. "All right!" she said, throwing her thought at him. "What are you going to do about Ken? You asked him to come."

"I've already talked with him about it. He understands. I told him we'd make him a reservation in Switzerland, too, if he could get off from his work."

"And did he say he could?"

"No. He said he couldn't take leave for that long."

"So away we go." Tippy pushed her paper aside and got up. "I think we're the limit," she exploded. "We don't give a hoot about what happens to six or seven other people, just so we can take Bobby on a trip. I've invited the Breitskis to supper, but that doesn't matter either, they can just stay in their own cold apartment. They only have two rooms and Marga hasn't any spot where she can entertain her soldier, so I said to bring him along, and. . . ." She stopped for lack of breath and because something caught in her throat, and her mother asked quickly:

"Darling, would it help you if we ask them to stay here while we're away? We could tell them we need to leave someone in the house, because we do, you know, and they would enjoy it. We could even leave the refrigerator stocked as their Christmas present."

"I guess so." Tippy knew she was beaten. The plans were made long before she had been consulted; and when her father said, "Come here, honey," she went to him reluctantly.

"Listen, Tip," he said, pulling her down on the arm of his chair. "We never do anything without thinking of you, don't you know that?" And she had to nod. "And if I were to tell you that this trip is for your own good," he went on, "would you believe me?"

"I don't quite see how I could," she mumbled.

"But would you?" He was so persistent with his question that she had to give in.

"I guess I'd try," she answered reluctantly.

"Then, do it. Believe me, Tippy, we're thinking more of you than of Bobby's vacation. We want you happy, honey. Please believe me."

"All right."

So she let them think she was happy. But when she escaped to her own room, she lay across her wide bed and wept. "They're thinking I've gone German," she sobbed. "They won't say so, but they think I fiddle around with Germans too much and wait for Ken to telephone and come down. They wish I'd be like Kay Macklin and play the field. They feel sorry for me and wish I could have a good time. As if I could have fun in Switzerland, with *Bobby!*"

She let tears soak into the counterpane and enjoyed the discomfort of having her cheek on a wet spot. And for several days the five o'clock hour had to take care of itself. She had no heart for the five o'clock hour and thought her father was better off without her doleful face. And then it was time for Bobby to come.

"Tip," her mother said, early that morning, "let's do our packing, so we won't be worried with it after Bobby gets here. You'll want to show him around tomorrow and we'll be leaving at the crack of dawn the next day, if I know Dad."

"Okay." Tippy dragged a suitcase down from the third floor and dumped her ski suit into it. "What sort of clothes shall I take?" she asked, standing in her mother's doorway."

"How about your navy blue wool?" Mrs. Parrish answered. "I thought it would be nice for evening and I looked for it because I have some extra room, but I couldn't find it. If you'll bring it to me, I'll pack it."

"I—I gave it away."

"You what?" Mrs. Parrish straightened up from the drawer she had bent over, and Tippy stammered again:

"I—I gave it to Marga."

"For goodness' sake, why?"

"Because she doesn't have much to wear."

"Oh, Tippy." Mrs. Parrish sighed and sat down on her bed. "There were a number of things I couldn't find," she said. "Have you given away everything you own?"

"Not much, but some. I just couldn't be comfortable when I looked so nice and other girls. . . ." She echoed her mother's sigh and went back to her room.

It seemed safer to put the hall between them, and she packed grimly while Mrs. Parrish sat on her bed and stared at the mountains, as if trying to see Bobby's plane and pull it along with her eyes.

Oh, Bobby, please hurry, Mrs. Parrish thought wildly. Three more hours to wait and I don't think I can keep a secret. I have half a notion to go in and tell her why we're going to Switzerland. She might rather have it to plan for than. . . . Oh, dear," she sighed. "Promises are so binding."

And Tippy folded her plaid dress for the suitcase and stood with the white wool in her hands. Why take it? Why subject it to a dull hotel and Bobby's indifference when it had enjoyed such wonderful week-ends? Why care? Her fingers lingered on the gold embroidery, and then with a shrug she doubled the dress over and slapped it in the case.

"I'm packed," she called, not knowing her mother still sat on her bed. "Shall we drive out to the air field, now?"

"No." Mrs. Parrish made a sudden show of being busy and answered, "Dad said the army pilot who's giving Bobby a lift will keep in touch with the field. He'll telephone us."

"Okay." Tippy wondered what she could do with a fragment of morning, and after wandering through the house, sat down at the desk in the living room and got out her writing portfolio. "I could write to Peter," she mumbled, looking through the number of letters she had begun and never finished, "or Alcie, perhaps. But I haven't anything to talk to them about, any more. I wonder if I ever will have."

She pushed the portfolio back into a drawer and spent the rest of the morning just staring out at the shining white world.

And it was almost one o'clock when Bobby Parrish jumped out of an army plane and loped toward his family. "Hi, ya!" he shouted, looking unusually tall in a new gray overcoat.

He wore no hat and his curly blond hair was too short to blow. His whole face was one wide grin as he hugged his mother, heartily pummeled his father, and gave Tippy's face a brotherly swipe with his hand that brought tears of pain to her eyes. "Oh, gosh," he said, "it's swell. Is this Garmisch?"

"It will be as soon as we get back into town," his mother answered, happy because college had done nothing to change him.

"Then let's get going. I'll drag out my duffle, and let's go."

"But what about the pilot, Bob?" his father asked. "I'll get your gear and ask him to ride in to town with us. Has he a place to stay while he's here?"

"He's going on to Munich." Bobby took his first real look at Tippy, said, "Well, you haven't changed much." Then he pointed out proudly, "It sure helps to have pals in the army. I ran into this character in Paris, after I got off the plane and was about to board the Orient Express, and we got to chinning. He told me he'd been on leave and had a flight to Munich coming up this morning, so we got off the train in some town where he stables his plane, and here we are. I don't know about army regulations, but I got here."

"I had them clear you." Colonel Parrish had returned with Bobby's aviator's bag, and he reproved, pleasantly, "It's a good thing I could. That flier's a nice kid and you might have landed him in trouble. Knowing you, you must have put on the pressure."

"Well, I did lay it on about my poor old sick mother," he admitted, winking at Mrs. Parrish. "Could I help it if he thought he ought to rush me to her deathbed? He darn near fell out of the plane when he saw you. But he rallied and asked if you were both my sisters and thought Tippy was the older one."

Bobby encircled his mother's waist and nuzzled his cold cheek against hers. "Gee, I've missed you, Mums," he said. "Nobody tucked me in at night or brought me a drink of water. They just yelled, 'Get to bed, Parrish, and cut out the noise.' Oh, yeah, I almost forgot. Pen sent you a letter. David and Carrol did, too, but Pen's weighed so much I'm lopsided from carrying it in my pocket."

He dropped one shoulder and managed to wrest his bag from his father without straightening up. And when he reached the house he ran upstairs and down so fast that he made Jochen look like a slow moving freight.

"You sure neglect your friends," he said severely to Tippy, when she sat in the living room with her mother and watched him display a surprising collection of neckties and gaudy wool socks. "Peter's the ghost of West Point, and Alcie never hears a word from you."

[121]

"She had you," Tippy returned saucily. "What does she want with letters from me when she has them from you? I don't see how you ever managed to tear yourself away and leave her."

"It just about killed me." Bobby's blue eyes twinkled and he held up his brightest pair of socks. "She knitted 'em," he said with great pride. "She knitted 'em for Peter to wear at home, on week-ends, but he didn't like his toes sticking out through the mistakes she made, so he gave 'em to me."

"And I suppose your toes stay in."

"They cuddle." Her sarcasm passed him by and he waved the socks around for his mother to see. "Alcie's my darling," he said blithely, and with complete frankness. "I may marry the lass about five years from now."

"I'll bet she won't wait for you." Tippy enjoyed a hollow laugh because she remembered a quarrel she and Alice had had over Bobby. "Once," she said, "I tried to make her promise to wait, and she wouldn't."

"Perhaps that was before she knew how wonderful I was." He was untouched, so confident, so smugly complacent that Tippy felt the old childish desire to get the better of him by fair means or foul. And they began a battle of words that sent her mother into gales of laughter, and made her almost as happy as she had been in her dear house on Governors Island.

"Oh, children, children," she pleaded, when Tippy had scored such a neat point that Bobby resorted to physical combat and pursued her around the room. "None of the *bric-a-brac* belongs to us. Be careful!"

The house was full of noise. It was like old times to see Tippy flying through the rooms with Bobby's new neckties streaming out behind her, to hear a racket above, followed by yelps for mercy. And when Colonel Parrish came home, Mrs. Parrish said to him, "You did have the right idea, Dave. It's working."

"Thank goodness for that." He stretched out in his favorite chair, and asked, "Where are they now?"

"Tippy took him out to see the town. And," she added happily, "they're probably staging a fight, right in the middle of Bahnhofstrasse."

CHAPTER X

"JUMPING JUPITER! I wish you would keep your big feet in your own half of the car." Tippy drew herself daintily into the corner and laid a protecting arm over the hat box that separated her from Bobby. "Can't you ever stay rightside up?"

"I'm hungry."

The Parrishes were on their way to Switzerland. The car was filled with boxes containing Christmas gifts, the luggage compartment was full of cases, and skis were tied to the ski rack on top. A large box of lunch took up space on the floor, and there was a continual rustle of waxed paper and the rattle of a thermos bottle as its cover was removed, used for a cup, and returned.

"Mums," Tippy complained, "he doesn't do anything but eat. And every time he eats, he moves everything off the box and pushes it over on me. He's just about ruined my best shoes."

"She shouldn't have worn 'em. Look at mine." Bobby endeavored to exhibit his sturdy footwear and brought forth a shriek.

"Children," Mrs. Parrish admonished in the traveling tone she had acquired years ago, "behave yourselves! Look at the marvelous scenery. These are the Alps you're seeing, and Dad says we're going through the pass in a few minutes. It isn't every day you can motor through Switzerland."

"No, thank goodness." Tippy leaned over to snatch the last ham sandwich and made a great show of hiding it behind her, then she suddenly bent to her *vis-à-vis* and whispered, "Bobby, do you want to go to Switzerland?"

"Sure, why not?"

"There's such a lot we could do in Garmisch. I wanted to take you to the Casa, and the Post Hotel, and to Riessersee to dinner, and have you meet the Vanderhoefs."

"We can do it when we get home. We'll only be gone a week and I'll have another week left over. Gee, I hope the hotel will provide a pretty girl for me to ski with."

Tippy hoped it would, too. Her awkward skiing would wreck Bobby's small stock of patience, and she preferred to fall down and get up alone to having him witness her clumsy progress. In fact, she planned to engage a professional instructor and to surprise Ken when they made their trip up the Kreuzeck. So she said fervently, "I do hope you'll find someone," and returned to her reverie.

The neat Swiss landscape flowed by. At first, the Parrishes rode through valleys that were dotted lightly with snow; but as the car began to climb, white giant mountains reared into the heavens, and by early evening they looked down on a world that was all white against a navy blue sky.

"There's our village," Colonel Parrish said triumphantly, stretching his tired back and pointing ahead. "We'll put the car in a garage there and a sleigh will meet us."

"How far do we go in a sleigh?" his wife asked.

"Just up the mountain a little way. I imagine the hotel's up where that bunch of lights is, just above the town. Can you see it?"

"Yes, and isn't it lovely?"

The car rolled through a quaint little village that was covered with snow. It was the cleanest snow Tippy had ever seen and it hung from gabled roofs like white cotton batting. Pink-cheeked children wore heavy coats with thick, bright mufflers tied around their necks, and knitted caps that had two little ears and made them look like dancing kittens.

Christmas Eve candles burned in almost every window; and people who hurried along the streets wore the happiness of a Yuletide spirit over their heavy clothes. It was a nice little town, and even without neon signs and lighted Christmas trees along its sidewalks, managed to be festive and gay.

Two sleighs stood before a fine copy of an American garage; and as Colonel Parrish slowed the car, one of the drivers got out, looking like a burly bear in his fur coat and cap. But he was an efficient bear, for in a very few minutes the four Parrishes were bundled under a pile of fur robes, and were going up the mountain to a cheerful jingle of bells while their luggage jingled just as musically behind them.

"Wow! Some hotel," Bobby praised, when they had stopped before a building with lights blazing from four tiers of windows, and porters had thrown back the robes and escorted them into a large lounge with a giant Christmas tree at one end of it. "This just suits me—if I can find my pretty girl."

He looked around eagerly, studying the people who were sitting on chairs and sofas; and, while she thought him a disloyal wretch, Tippy looked with him. She saw dark, richly paneled walls; strong, comfortable furniture, and the largest fireplace she had ever beheld. Logs, as long as small trees, were burning brightly in it and a group of people in ski clothes reached barely to the top of its wide red mouth.

"Don't see any pretty girls, yet, do you?" Bobby whispered, in such an urgent voice that she turned on him.

"Honestly," she cried, "you make me tired! All day yesterday you couldn't talk of anyone but Alcie. You simply crammed her down my throat. And now, hardly twenty-four hours later, you're hunting someone else. Well, take that one over there. The dark-haired one with her back to us. She's all alone. If you whistle through your teeth, I have no doubt she'll turn around and stare at you."

"Okay, I guess I will." Bobby followed his words with

such a shrill fife that she jumped away and tried to pretend she had come in alone.

And of course, the girl turned. Everyone in the room turned, but it was only the brown haired girl whom Tippy saw. "Alcie! Alcie!" she shrieked, making far more noise than Bobby had done, and starting across the thick rugs with her arms outflung.

The two ran together like an answer to the arithmetical problem of two trains coming from opposite directions at the same rate of speed. Brown hair and tan curls bumped. The arms of a leopard coat and a green ski suit were all mixed up and not even Bobby could untangle them.

"Hey!" he reminded. "Let go. I found the girl."

"You did not." Tippy pulled Alice Jordon down on a sofa and ignored him. "Oh, Alcie," she breathed with a sigh of pure joy, "tell me, how did you get here?" And she went on before Alice could answer, "It's the craziest thing I ever heard of. It can't be true, can it?"

"I hope it is." Alice's small face was as excited as Tippy's. Her brown hair hung around it, just as straight and glossy as ever, and she said, her gray eyes shining, "I brought Bitsy and Donny over to spend the winter with Jenifer. Ever since Jenifer married Cyril, Bitsy hasn't been happy. She. . . ."

"But that's in England," Tippy interrupted, puzzled. "You're *here*."

"Jenifer and Cyril dropped me off on their way to Italy." Alice tucked one foot under her and slid around on the sofa. That way she could see Bobby, too, for he had squeezed in on what was left of a cushion and she could look at him over Tippy's shoulder. "This is the way it was," she said. "I'd better begin at the beginning or we'll never get straight. We all missed Jenifer terribly after she got married and went away this fall, but Bitsy was so little when Mother died that Jenifer really was her mother. She wouldn't eat and she got so terribly thin that Dad said—I guess Jenifer was about as

[127]

lonesome as Bitsy, way off in a strange country—Dad said he wished he had some way to get her over there for a visit."

"And you offered to bring her."

"No, it wasn't exactly like that." Alice shook her head until her hair swung back and forth, and hurried on, "You know, Cyril's sister was killed in an air raid, and his older brother was, too. His mother's still an invalid from it, and Cyril thought it would give her something to do if she had Bitsy to fuss over; so he and Jenifer wrote to ask if Bits could come there and live. And then, Donny wanted to go. Cyril's his hero and he doesn't do so well without Jenifer, either."

The Jordon household was such a complicated one that Tippy nodded. She knew it contained four sets of children, and ranged from own sisters and brothers, through half-sisters and brothers, through step-sisters and brothers, all the way to Donny who was simply an extra. Donny was only a nephew whose parents had been killed in an accident. So, familiar with the relation of each child to the other eight, she prodded Alice on by asking, "How did you happen to be the one who brought them?"

"Well," Alice stopped and considered. "Of course, I wanted to," she said, "but I thought Gwen had first right, because she's the oldest, now, except Peter who can't get out of the Point. But she didn't want to. She could have come during her vacation from college, but she's in love with a dud at the Point. And I do mean dud, don't I, Bobby?"

"He's a mess." Bobby gave her confirmation and a signal to go on, so she cried: "So, I got it! I actually got it. We came over in style on the Queen Elizabeth, with some people Dad knew, and Lady Carlington is so crazy about Bitsy and so keen on finding a tutor for Donny that Jenifer and Cyril decided to take the wedding trip they never did get, and I. . . ." Alice fell over on Tippy and they clung together until Tippy sat up and said:

"Great shades of cousin Carrie, I can't believe it!" She sat up only because Bobby pulled on the back of her coat. It was either relieve the strain or wear a leopard with a gaping wound, and she commanded, "Let go of me. This was Penny's best coat last winter and I have to wear it for years." And she listened to Alice tell gayly:

"Your father cabled Bobby about this trip. Bobby cabled me, I asked Jenifer and cabled Bobby, he cabled your father again, and . . . oh, we've spent so much money trying to surprise you. And I can stay all the time you're here and you'll drop me off in St. Moritz on your way back!"

She stopped to breathe, and Bobby managed to toss in, "She didn't deserve it. She's been so grouchy over coming that if I'd been Mums and Dad, I'd have called it off or left her at home."

"Huh!" Tippy brushed him aside with a shrug, since he had no physical hold on her now, and seeing her parents crossing the lounge, jumped up and ran to meet them. "Bless you, darlings, bless you!" she cried, hugging them and not noticing that the Parrishes were providing interesting drama for everyone in the room.

American, French and British, relaxing after a day on the ski runs, lazily watched the latest arrivals and speculated about them. Four had come in together, yet one was being embraced again, and the pretty girl under a straight brown bang was the center of attention.

"Probably another daughter back from school," a wind-reddened Britisher told his curious wife, but she shook her head and answered, "They don't look alike. Four do, but one doesn't." And she tuned her hearing aid higher to listen to the blond girl cry:

"And we're going to room together! Oh, joy!"

"They're just friends," she boomed, in the loud voice of the deaf, and making Mrs. Parrish turn and smile at her.

"And they haven't seen each other for several months," Mrs. Parrish explained, laughing a little while she started her flock toward the elevators. "That accounts for the noise. It was a surprise for my daughter."

The elevator was a fancy, glass affair that crept up slowly. The Parrishes were still novelties in a cage, and until they disappeared from view, eyes followed them and Bobby growled, "Stand still, Tip. You made 'em think we're morons."

"I didn't whistle—you did," she reproved righteously. "That's what started them staring at us." And when the elevator stopped at a floor, she brushed by him and sailed out. "Alcie and I'll see you at dinner," she said over her shoulder, not looking to see which way he turned in the corridor and blocking his last look at Alice who was fitting her key in a lock. "But you may stop by for us and we'll go down with you."

"Why, thanks, that's big of you."

Tippy followed her roommate into a chintz-and-maple room that had twin beds. Casement windows looked out on a star-studded sky, and she said, "It doesn't seem a bit like Christmas Eve, does it?"

"No, and I was terribly afraid I'd be homesick. When Jenifer left me this morning, I began thinking, what if you shouldn't get here and what would I do, all alone? But it's all right, now."

"All right? Why, as Penny used to say, 'It's practically perfect.'" Tippy tossed her coat on one bed and flung herself on the other. "Oh, Alcie," she groaned, "this has been the longest almost-four months I've ever spent. You just can't imagine how terrible Germany looks."

"Yes, I can. England's no prize."

"But the people! They're so frightfully depressing that I've given away a lot of my clothes and Mums thinks I've lost my mind. Maybe I would have," she said, sighing, "if it hadn't been for Ken."

"Oh, my soul, how is Ken?" Alice sat down on the bed, too,

tucked her feet under her and prepared for confidences. "You never did write a thing about him," she prodded when Tippy was dramatically silent. "I might have thought he fell off the boat except there wasn't anything about it in the *Army and Navy Journal*. Do you ever see him?"

"Oh, yes, often, on week-ends." Tippy slid back and propped herself against the headboard. "He's been so wonderful to me. I—uh—I. . . ." She looked dreamily at the dim figure on the other end of the bed, and murmured, "I just discovered today—I'm in love."

Her words struck Alice right in the chest, like a rocket. She never had heard them used except in plays and movies; for not even Jenifer, who certainly adored her Cyril, had expressed her tenderness so dramatically. Gwenn was constantly "swooning with *amour*" for her cadet, and "beside myself over the guy," but not even she ever had made such a forthright statement; and Tippy went completely out of focus while she cried in shocked surprise, "You must have gone crazy! The idea of being in love at your age! Did the stupe ask you to marry him?"

"Oh, he doesn't know it." Tippy sat up and retracted at least half of her implication. "He's just been awfully sweet to me and tries to think up things to do to make me happier. Perhaps he does it because of Mums and Dad. I don't know. He likes me all right," she said, trying to remember when Ken had considered her an equal in age, and failing. "He's just sweet, and kind," she finished lamely.

"Then you've just got a bad case of hero worship." Alice decided the matter and jerked her head in a quick nod that settled it, at least so far as she was concerned. "You wouldn't be in such a silly state if you had some boys your own age to go around with," she decided sensibly. "You don't want to be —be in love with a man his age, do you?"

"Well, of course, I do, Alcie, if he could love me in return. We could have a beautiful life together."

"And what would you do with Peter? My goodness," Alice reminded, "he offered you his A pin, and everything. He practically told you he wanted to marry you, someday."

Tippy wished she hadn't been so quick to confide Peter's slip of the tongue to his sister. Even Peter admitted it to have been a slip, one little sentence that had grown into pages and pages of letters, and she returned hopefully, "He has two more years at the Point. He may fall in love with someone else."

"Not Peter. Once you tried to make me promise I'd marry Bobby and you'd marry Peter. You said you liked him better than any boy you knew, and. . . ."

"I didn't know Ken then. Oh, Alcie." Tippy rested her elbows on her knees and cupped her cheeks in her hands. "Things do get mixed up, I know they do. I wouldn't ever have a chance to marry Ken if I wanted to. I know I wouldn't, because there are several American girls his age in Munich and he must know dozens at home. If you had to live in this depressing place you'd understand why he's nice to me, why he just thinks, poor little Tippy. He couldn't ever fall in love with me, Alcie, so don't worry."

Alice looked along the bed and wondered. Tippy's curls were mussed and her mouth curved in a very kissable way; and, thought she, had she been Peter Jordon instead of Alice, she would be most uneasy about Ken Prescott. But aloud, she only said, "Look. It must be nearly seven o'clock, and we're due downstairs at seven. I'll have to change. We can talk tonight, when we come to bed."

"All right." Tippy got up reluctantly. Having confessed to an unsuspected love, she would have enjoyed mulling over the pros and cons of the situation for at least an hour longer, but Alice had pulled off her bright, nitted ski socks and was unbuttoning her green jacket. Alice had excitement waiting for her downstairs in the uninspiring form of Bobby, and was saying with great haste and little consideration:

[132]

"Stop worrying about Ken for tonight. Cyril arranged with the manager to bring a Christmas tree to your mother and father's room. It's a little one but it has real candles on it, and we'll have fun. I brought my box from home with me."

"But I haven't anything to give you," Tippy discovered sadly. "I sent it to the States."

"You thought you did. Your mother has it." Alice chose a new red dress from a hanger on a clothes rack and with it in her hands, said, "Stop worrying, Tip. Haven't you ever learned that you worry and fuss over things, and then always come out on top?"

CHAPTER XI

TIPPY considered Alice's words of three days ago. If her spirits weren't exactly on top, her body certainly was. It was on top of the world. A white world that looked like a great cone of whipped cream. She had got up there by clinging to a tow rope and would have to get down by a mixture of balance, gravity, and two unreliable pieces of wood. And she was quite alone with her problem.

"You've had an instructor for two whole days," Bobby had reminded her only that morning, when she had shouldered her skis and was passively waiting for the pleasant young Swiss who was to make up their foursome. "I told him you'd try it alone. I'll help you," he hurriedly added, when she sat down on a bench and looked as permanent as a manikin in a store window. "Alcie and I'll both help you, and anyway, you're getting pretty good, now."

And the way he had helped was by being angry when she unexpectedly fell down and lost one of her skis over a ledge of rock. Of course, Tippy reflected, standing alone in her white world, he had hit his lip on a pipe when he slid down for the ski and had coasted farther than she liked to remember with a lot of mountain rolling along with him; but he had climbed safely back. Nothing was lost but his temper and a piece out of his father's old cavalry breeches. He had returned her ski, but he slapped it down in the snow and left her to clop-clop along behind while he and Alice took merry little slides across gullies, or poled their way around rising curves.

Alice had tried to wait; in all fairness, Tippy acknowledged she had. But it is impossible to wait for someone who refuses to catch up, who even branches off in another direction. Tippy had stopped every few strides to consider the view, and had loitered behind until a curve cut her off from the safe, well-marked trail. Then, without knowing she was going to do it, she had suddenly tossed back her head and struck off in an uncharted direction.

And here she was. It had taken at least two hours to get here. Two hours of clinging to cliffs, of crawling and groping ahead for flaws in the snow, of taking a fall that was far worse than Bobby's, and being saved from a plunge down the mountain by having her ski stick in the snow and act as a brake. Somehow, she had moved along through fear and had managed to come out on the bottom of a ski trail, and the beautiful sight of people.

And she was still wondering why she had grasped a loop on the cable.

"Here you are, Miss," a ruddy man had said, stepping back and letting her have the strap as it went by. "Up you go." And without even stopping to rest, up she went.

For some reason, in her tiredness, she had expected to find Bobby at the top. He would be waiting there with a frightened Alice, and she would wearily give him a piece of her mind. But he wasn't there. No one was there whom she knew, and she lurched away from the cable and stood on shaking legs. She was still standing. Men had come up and swooped down again like birds, and it was only after a half hour of anxiously scanning the peaks around her that she realized she was lost on a strange ski trail. It was a steeper and slicker run than any she had attempted as yet, and she wondered wretchedly, if she ought to wait until everyone went home to luncheon, then sit down and somehow scoot back to the bottom, again.

She had been so hot after her trek and from clinging to the moving cable without falling down that her body prickled and her scalp tingled; but after she had stood so long she began to grow clammy and cold. Just to look at so much snow made her shiver. She pulled her parka closer around her face and buttoned a flap that covered her chin. Three men were left against the ragged timberline of fir trees far below her and she wanted to wait until they shoved their poles into the snow and slid out of sight. But they took such an endless time lighting their cigarettes. Her teeth chattered like a bag of marbles, and when she could bear it no longer, she took off her skis, set them side by side, and sat down on them.

It was an ignominious descent. Sometimes she was on top and sometimes her skis were, but she managed to use her poles for brakes and took the last part of the trail on her stomach. There, the ground settled into a long, gentle slope that went far past the timber line, and she would have enjoyed doing that part standing up if her legs had been stronger, or if it had been the end of her journey. She still had a long trip home. Where and in what direction was a mystery, but she had hope of sliding down to flat terrain and finding a lodge or a road.

She was hot again. She was hot and prickly as she scrambled up and buckled her tired feet into her ski straps, so she unfastened her coat. Her poles bit into the snow and she shot off with a jerk. All the muscles had melted out of her legs and even the bones were rubber. Whatever she had learned flew out of her head, so that she jerked and lurched and often fell down. But at last she came to a road. It was the most welcome road she ever had seen for it had prints of runners on it and countless nicks from horses' hoofs, and from not too far away came the cheerful jingle of approaching sleigh bells.

Tippy fell down on a bank beside the road and waited. She left her skis where she had stumbled out of them and leaned wearily on her poles. And when two brown horses jogged musically around a turn, she wondered how she could ever stand up and ask for directions. But the sleigh stopped of its own accord and a driver from her own hotel looked down at her.

"Are you going back, *ma'mselle?*" he asked, and she could only nod.

She had no breath for speaking, and he sized up her plight for himself as he wrapped his reins around the whip socket and got down. "Ah, you are veree late for ze luncheon," he said, cheerfully, picking up her skis and standing them in the sleigh. "Now I take ze poles." He unclamped her red mittens from their grip and lifted her in his arms.

"Up you go," he said, depositing her on the back seat and tucking a bear robe around her.

It was the second time Tippy had heard the same sentence, but now it sounded more musical than the bells that followed it. She leaned her head against the shaggy rug behind her and closed her eyes. She had been afraid. Now she knew it. She had been terribly afraid all morning. She had been lost in the Alps, clinging to crags and skirting crevasses. She had blundered on because she was afraid to stop, afraid to stay where she was, perhaps to freeze. Bobby wouldn't have cared, but her mother and father would have missed her if she had frozen to death. Perhaps they were frightened even now. Two tears squeezed out and she asked weakly, "What time is it?"

"Almost three o'clock. You are hungry, *ma'mselle?*"

"No—yes, I guess so." Tippy decided she was hungry. She was alive and hungry. It was a wonderful feeling and she cuddled down inside the fur to enjoy it.

But back in the hotel, her family had no such joyous emotions. They hovered near the door where they could watch both the road and the desk clerk as he telephoned the different hotels and ski lodges; and Mrs. Parrish asked again, "Bobby, are you sure Tippy couldn't have fallen over a cliff when she was behind you?"

"No, really she couldn't have, Mrs. Parrish," Alice answered for him, her face worried and her cheeks streaked from crying. The last time I saw her we were crossing a wide place and we sort of swung around a curve and waited. We waited and waited. And when I went back, she wasn't anywhere at all." Alice was loath to say that her return for Tippy had been delayed by an argument with Bobby because he refused to go with her. But some sort of explanation was necessary, and she reluctantly added, "After awhile, he came, too, but we couldn't find her. Bobby decided she'd gone back home."

"So he put her out of his mind." Colonel Parrish looked stern and Bobby mumbled:

"I—I guess I did, Dad. I was mad at her, but you know nothing ever happens to Tip."

"So far, it hasn't, but there's always a first time. Tippy was in your care." And with that blunt admonition he opened the door and went outside.

"Dave," Mrs. Parrish called, running after him, "you don't really think anything has happened to Tippy, do you?"

"No, darling, I don't," he answered, fastening her coat tighter around her throat, then slipping his arm through hers. "But if Tip doesn't show up pretty soon I'm going to call out whatever they call out around here and start a search. Bobby and Alcie have been back for more than an hour and she's had plenty of time to come home."

"Perhaps she joined another crowd of skiers and. . . ." Mrs. Parrish's words trailed off, and he propped them up by finishing heartily:

"I'm sure she did. A lot of people from the hotel stayed at the shelter for lunch and no doubt she's with them. Here comes one of our sleighs and I think I'll ask the driver to take me out on a tour with him."

It was of no use to remind her that a skier might easily break an ankle or that the mountains were full of treacherous, snow-covered drops cut in the rock. Trails were laid out and skiers were supposed to stick to the trails. So he held up a hand and stopped the sleigh as it jingled along the driveway.

"Wait, driver," he called. "I'd like you to take me back to the hotel's ski lodge."

"Yes, *monsieur.*" The sleigh stopped and the horses shook themselves in a musical cascade. "As soon as I deliver my passenger," the driver answered. "You wait, *monsieur,* I come right back."

Colonel Parrish looked at the empty sleigh. There was a mound of fur on the back seat, but no passenger. Just a mound of fur that looked like a headless bear with one red paw. "She sleep," the driver explained, his eyes twinkling. "She very tired. She sleep." And Colonel Parrish sprang forward.

"I have her, Marge," he shouted, peeling back the fur like a flap on an envelope and exposing Tippy's flushed cheeks. And then he looked up and grinned. "She's mine," he explained, into the interested face above him. "We lost her."

"*Oui.*" The old mountaineer had delivered strange passengers, but never one quite so young and pretty, and he smiled through his giant moustache. "She very tired," he repeated. "Climb much I zink. Oop and down."

"Yes, she's been at it for six hours."

Colonel and Mrs. Parrish provided a happy escort as the sleigh went to the hotel steps, and Mrs. Parrish said: "It seems a shame to wake her." But as Bobby and Alice hurtled through the door, she added gently, "Poor little thing." And she gave Tippy a reluctant shake. "Honey," she whispered, leaning over to kiss Tippy's cheek that was hot and creased from the rough lining of the robe, "you're home, now."

"Ugh." Tippy blinked and swallowed. Then she gave a wriggle and burrowed down again.

"Tippy," Alice coaxed from the other side of the sleigh. "Hi. Can't you wake up?"

"I don't want to go down the slide. Hunhuh."

"But you're home. We're waiting to have lunch with you. Tip. . . ." Alice's brown little hand reached out and smoothed Tippy's damp curls back from her forehead. "Please wake up," she begged.

"Huh? Oh, my soul, where am I?" Tippy sat up straight

and blinked. "Well, how do you do?" she said, trying to focus her eyes. And she added unnecessarily, "I guess I went to sleep."

"You must have." Her father laid back the rest of the robes and she stood up in the sleigh and stretched.

"I feel fine," she said, "after my nap. But, boy, oh, boy, was I tired!" and her eyes landed on Bobby.

He had kept himself well in the background, dreading the moment when she was bound to discover him, but at the scathing look she shot him, he came manfully forward and lifted her down. "Okay, Tip," he said with his arms still around her, "I'm sorry. You scared us to death."

"I should hope so." She saw his bruised lip that looked as if a bee had stung him, and offered her forgiveness. "But don't get so mad, next time," she snapped, "and don't always be wishing you could go off and leave me. Alcie's my guest, too, and I'm getting kind of tired of feeling like I'm just tagging along. Being a third is no fun."

And she spoke of that again when she was upstairs alone with him and Alice. She was in a warm woolen bathrobe and they had finished a combination lunch and afternoon tea and pushed the table outside.

"I don't like never having anybody to do things with," she complained. "Not that I have to have a date every minute of my life, but I've been kind of an extra ever since we got here."

"I brought you a guy to dance with last night," Bobby said lazily, from the one comfortable chair. "I thought the look you gave him was going to sizzle him right down to a cinder."

"A fifteen-year old child!" she scoffed. "He reached about to the tip of my nose. Oh," she added before he could speak, "I know it was the best you could do. I'm not expecting you to find me a man when they're aren't any. I'm only asking you to behave yourself when I have to be with you."

"Okay. It's hard, but I'll try." Bobby got up and strolled to the door. And with the knob in his hand, turned to invite generously, "You can come down when Alcie does and I'll buy you a cup of Swiss hot chocolate with whipped cream. One cup," he added, not caring if he spoiled his exit. "If there's a second round, it can be on you."

He ambled out and Tippy frowned at Alice. "Now, do you see what I mean?" she fumed. "Every time he's nice, he wrecks it. And right after I'd forgiven him for bringing that pimply little creature up to dance with me, too. Oh, well," she shrugged her shoulders and curled up in the chair he had left. "Bobby's just a child, and I suppose I'm spoiled because I've been going around with a man who does things right."

"Peter does things right, too," Alice reminded in a small, loyal voice. "He spent a lot of money on you."

"I don't mean money." Tippy frowned and said carefully, "Peter *is* nice, Alcie. I like him, I really do, but. . . ." Now was the time to introduce Ken Prescott again and continue the one-sided confidence of their first evening together, and she explained, "I'm not going to see Peter for ages. I can't just go on living on the *memory* of the way he did things."

"No, I suppose you can't."

Alice agreed reluctantly, for Peter had told her the same thing late one blustery afternoon when he was lounging before a glowing fire in the Jordon library. Hands clasped around one knee of his gray cadet trousers, he had said earnestly, "I guess I won't be making much time with Tippy from here on, Alcie. She'll meet a lot of other guys over there and . . . well, the hottest letter-writer can't compete with the Joe who's on the spot. But you might keep my memory green, if you ever get a chance."

Firelight touched him with a warm red glow that brought out color and shadows. It brightened his short hair to the yellow of ripe wheat, smoothed the thin plane of his cheekline and firm chin, and cut sharply across his gray uniform and a corner of the green chair behind him. Alice had wished she could snap a picture of him to carry to Tippy, but at that moment he had unclasped his knee and leaned back into obscurity.

"I never like to write that I go stag to the dances," he went on. "It makes me sound as faithful as a St. Bernard. But if you should ever see Tip over there, you might casually mention that when I do have a drag, it's only some femme Gwen brings along with her and soon forgotten. I guess I'm a constant guy," he had ended, from the shadows that engulfed him.

Alice thought about that last afternoon and Peter's sober entreaty, and she said unexpectedly from her perch on the bed, "Peter's awfully popular at the Point. Of course, he seldom drags the same girl twice, but I guess he's like you are— he can't just sit around, thinking."

A moment of silence followed her words. Every feature on Tippy's face registered surprise, all the way from her parted lips to a crease across her forehead, and she said with reluctance, "Why, I thought . . . he never mentions any girls in his letters."

"Well, he wouldn't." Alice's own gray eyes widened and she exclaimed briskly, "Peter wouldn't flaunt his popularity. And anyway, I don't think he realizes how crazy girls are about him. You know, he just goes along, being Peter." And let that sink in, she thought, watching Tippy and vowing to coach her brother when she got home. "He wasn't even spoiled over all the fuss the newspapers made about him as a football find," she flung in for good measure.

"Well." Tippy silently considered Peter, and it was as if Alice had brought her a photograph, after all. Not the serious one in the firelight, but a newspaper shot of Peter racing for a touchdown before a grandstand full of girls. "Well," she said again, "you never know about people, do you—really?"

"Hunuh." Alice shook her head. "And now, about Ken," she suggested. But Tippy jumped up and walked to the window.

"I hate it over here, Alcie," she muttered, looking unseeingly at the beautiful world beyond the cold glass. "Honestly, I do. I'm always lonesome, just like today—always tagging along as an extra. Ken understands about it, but I never thought Peter would."

"Oh, Peter understands a lot."

"I suppose so." She stared at the white mountains for a moment before she said slowly, "I'll write to Peter tonight and thank him for the kodak book and the West Point compact. Even if he isn't very serious about things, he keeps saying he thinks I'm wonderful. Ken understands what a bad spot I'm in and he tries to help me, but I don't mean a thing to him. He doesn't really see me. Yes," she sighed again and turned back to the room, "you and Bobby can dance and I'll come up and write a letter to Peter."

But it was a hard letter to write. There was Peter, running up and down a football field with a ball tucked under his arm or surrounded by a ring of beautiful girls; and here was she, completely alone and not fully appreciated by even one second lieutenant. Tippy sucked her pen and spent more time pulling the paper forward and pushing it back than she did writing.

"What good would a letter be, anyway?" she mused woefully. Peter could only read it between classes and dash off a return about his work and the weather. He would never tell her about the girls he took to hops, and there was no reason for her to write long accounts of the desolate Germans and the help she was trying to give them. Why should Peter care if the Breitskis received coffee every afternoon, or that she had found two tires for Jochen's battered bicycle and medicine for a child with a stomach ailment? That she had given a birthday party for Annie's little niece? Peter was busy. And she laid down her pen and sat twisting the ring on her finger, flipping it back and forth and watching its seal catch the light from her desk lamp.

"Blast it," she muttered, listening to voices at the elevator, laughing, chattering voices. "I'm lonesome."

She shoved back her chair and went over to consider herself in the mirror on the sturdy dresser. As a rule, Tippy only looked at herself when she was dressing, and it seemed heartless to stand staring at someone who looked so young and desolate without offering a bit of comfort, and she turned abruptly away and flung herself on the bed.

It had been such a long, hard day, this fourth day of her holiday in Switzerland, and she was so physically tired that even her morose thoughts scattered like sheep wandering away from a flock; and though she kept collecting them and dragging them back, her eyelids drooped. Finally she abandoned the chase and was relaxed in even breathing when the telephone rang.

The telephone sat in a high metal cradle on a night stand beside her bed and made a great clatter when she fumbled sleepily for it. "Hello," she said in a rather grumpy voice, thinking it was inconsiderate of Jenifer to put in her nightly check on Alice just when she had forgotten her troubles; but Ken's deep voice rumbled brightly back at her.

"Hi, cherub," he answered, as clearly as if he were in the room with her. "How's everything?"

"Oh. Oh—fine!" she exclaimed, rolling over and clutching the receiver as though it held a fortune.

"Is the skiing good?"

"Simply marvelous." Up to now, the skiing had been her greatest disappointment, but in the excitement of hearing Ken's voice, she almost bubbled over in her enthusiasm. "I was out all day today," she told him breathlessly. "I got lost and fell down mountains and almost scared the family and myself to death."

"All alone?"

"Umhum."

"Gosh, that's not so good." There was a pause, then he asked anxiously, "How would you like to have a companion?"

"Do you mean . . ."

"I got four days' leave and I'm almost there. I thought I could make it tonight but a pass is blocked and I have to go back and around another way. I'll start out at the crack of dawn and I should pull in before noon—if you want me to."

"Oh, Ken!" Tippy started a gay, glad laugh and ended in choking; so he went on:

"Can you get me a room?"

"Of course. The hotel's practically empty because no one has any money except Americans. The Britishers and French had to go home right after Christmas and I guess the Swiss see enough mountains." She knew she was prattling, so settled the matter by simply saying, "Or you can room with Bobby."

"Right. Don't go off where I can't find you."

"Oh, I won't. I'll be right here. But hurry."

"Sure will. Good night."

Tippy laid the telephone back into its uncomfortable cradle. It was such a precious thing that she adjusted it carefully before she spun to the glass again and looked at her smiling self. "Hi, cherub," she caroled.

Her comb flew through her curls and lipstick went on with a sweep. People and laughter were waiting downstairs, and she decided to dance with the pimply boy, should he ask her. She would even buy Bobby a sandwich. With her purse tucked under her arm, she skipped to the door. Her dismal, unfinished letter to Peter lay on the desk and she snatched it up as she passed it. It made a soft crackling ball when she crumpled it up and aimed it at the waste basket.

"I'll do better by you, tomorrow, bud," she promised. Then she whirled across the hall and punched out "Happy days are here again" on the elevator bell.

CHAPTER XII

TIPPY rode in the sleigh to meet Ken. She was afraid the driver might miss him or that Ken would drive through the village and attempt the mountain in his car, so she started early and spent an hour in quaint little curio shops. And just when she was having a small carved bear boxed to mail to Davy, the shop door flew open and Bobby bounced in.

"Hello," he greeted cheerfully, "Alcie's down the line, buying some stuff. We walked down and have been looking for you. Thought we'd ride back."

He looked overjoyed to find her, quite as if he hadn't seen her for days, and Tippy had to laugh. "It makes a great difference when you don't have to be with me, doesn't it?" she remarked wisely, paying her Swiss francs and taking her small package by a wooden peg thrust through the string. "I'll teach you a lesson in manners by being polite and saying I'm glad you came."

"I should think you would be." Bobby was not in the least chagrined, and he pointed out, "I know Ken better than you do."

"Oh, no, my friend." She smiled an inarticulate farewell to the shopkeeper and added, as Bobby held open the door for her, "You might have, when we were on Governors Island, but not now. Remember, he's been the only man I've had dates with, in Germany."

"Well, don't get too serious about him. He's not in your age-bracket." Bobby swung along the snow-covered sidewalk beside her, and snatching a glance at him without turning her head, Tippy wondered how much of her conversation with

Alice had been passed on. But he said no more. Musical cigarette boxes interested him and he pulled her to a stop before a window that had a display of watches and clocks.

Much to her surprise, he behaved as an older brother should; and when Ken's car was flagged down, she had to admit he made the greetings easier. Ever since she had put her sentimental feelings into words, she had been uneasy. The three little words stated such a pertinent fact. They made her stand out from Alice who had never uttered them and put her in a class of older girls. She could have said, 'I'm mad about him,' or 'crazy about him,' or used a dozen different expressions that would have meant nothing at all and would have left her free to face him without the knowledge that Alice's wide gray eyes were fixed on her.

And of course, Ken treated them all alike. He was so happy to see them all that Alice's face expressed silent, sad sympathy when he swung her up in the sleigh beside Tippy and climbed in between them. He was impartial in his division of the fur robe, too, and in spite of loyalty to Peter, she was willing him to tuck an extra inch or so around Tippy or to give her one special, fond glance. But he failed to do either, and she sighed so loudly that Bobby turned around from the front seat and stared.

"You silly," Tippy exploded, when they were finally up the mountain and she could pull Alice aside in the hotel lounge and scold her. "If you don't stop looking at Ken, then at me, at Ken and back at me, you're going to have him thinking you're touched in the head."

"You said he isn't in love with you and I wanted to find out if he is," Alice defended. "He isn't."

"I know it. I told you that much, and if it doesn't bother me and I can manage to have a good time in spite of it, it seems to me that you could. He came all the way to Switzerland, didn't he?"

"Yes, but maybe he wanted to ski."

"Oh, Alcie, you're such a lamb." Tippy's heart spilled out tenderness like a broken water pitcher. "I'm just having fun because he's here," she said, not being entirely truthful but making Alice give a relieved smile. "I have someone to go around with. Forget what I said the other night, pet, because I do get off the beam, you know."

"All right."

The next two days in Switzerland were everything the brochures promised. Tippy had a skiing partner who laughed when she fell down and then picked her up and dusted her off and, best of all, who praised her. She had a dancing partner much smoother than Bobby and not so quarrelsome. Ken whirled her around a tiled floor in a softly lighted, oak-trimmed retreat that was a cross between a Swiss chalet and a cuckoo clock; and she thought they were almost as good together as the Vanderhoefs. And he was so contagiously enthusiastic that Tippy's cheeks were constantly flushed and her eyes sparkled like topazes.

Clothes flew in all directions in the room she shared with Alice, for ski suits were jerked off and sweaters and skirts pulled on. The white wool almost hopped off its hanger when she banged the door and reached for it with eager fingers, and the top of the dresser was littered with everything from wet wool socks to bobby pins.

"I have to hurry," Tippy muttered on their last afternoon and stamping her foot into an Oxford that was still stiff from drying on a radiator. "I'm meeting Ken for a sandwich in ten minutes. Do you want us to order something for you and Bobby?"

"No, thanks." Alice was struggling with a zipper that had caught, and she mumbled through set lips, "We're going down to the village in the sleigh. Bobby—drat this thing—said he'd have the car checked for your father. There." She gave the stubborn zipper a jerk and made a face when it slid as smoothly up her green skirt as if it had never been off its track. "But we'll meet you for dinner. I've got to run."

The door slammed behind her, then opened again for her to release the chunk of flying fur coat it had tried to bite off, and Tippy hopped on one foot to her other shoe. "Just one more evening," she groaned. "Oh, I wish I could hurry faster."

She tied her shoe lace and twisted around to inspect her stocking seams. They were straight and her face passed inspection, so she was only a few minutes behind Alice as she ran down two flights of stairs. But the quaint little retreat was empty. Even the waiter was taking a nap against a wainscoted wall. He was a tired, dispirited waiter and she hated to wake him. But when she pulled out a carved oak chair he came to of his own accord and sprang over to her.

"Two chicken sandwiches, please," she ordered, "and two pots of chocolate with a big bowl of whipped cream." Then she wondered if she should sit where she was or go out through the lobby in search of Ken.

Ken had ridden down in the elevator. Not having as much to do to his person as Tippy, he had changed into slacks, a tweed jacket and sweater, and had been in the glass cage when it stopped for Alice.

"Tip isn't quite ready," she told him, as he walked across the lounge with her to Bobby, and so, seeing Colonel Parrish sitting in one of the deep chairs before the fireplace, he had strolled on over.

"You're just the fellow I wanted to see," Colonel Parrish said, looking up with a welcome and laying his book on a low table beside him. "Are you having a good time?"

"Swell, sir." Ken dropped into a comfortable chair on the other side of the table and held out his cigarette case.

But Colonel Parrish shook his head. "Thanks, I have one,"

he answered, waving at an ash tray where a spiral of smoke drifted up. Then he leaned back and asked abruptly, "Ken, what's your opinion of Tippy?"

"Sir?" The question was so unexpected that Ken stopped crossing one knee over the other and let his foot slide back as it was. "I don't believe I quite understand, sir," he said.

"Then, let me explain." Colonel Parrish took off his glasses and rubbed his eyes and forehead with a weary gesture. "You know Tippy about as well as anyone could, right now," he began. "What she's like and how deeply she feels about things. Her mother and I are worried," he said frankly. "We brought her over here because we thought she'd have a good time, but it isn't working out that way. Her school's wrong, she's lonely, and, worst of all, she's carried away by the condition of the country and the people. She's talked quite a bit to you about that, hasn't she?"

"Yes sir, but I hoped she was getting better about it." Ken lighted a cigarette and finished crossing his knees. "Has she told you about the dragon?" he asked.

"No, what's that?"

"She's got the idea that some sort of dragon's devouring Europe. Of course, it's just a simile and Tippy's quaint little way of expressing things, but she has something there. That's one reason I introduced her to the Vanderhoefs." He watched his own thin thread of smoke as it drifted slowly toward the draft in the fireplace and said, "They're doing a fine job for a lot of people, but they're sane about it. Jeannie keeps her own family life apart and her viewpoint clear."

"But she has a family life," Colonel Parrish pointed out. "Tippy's lonely."

"I know that, sir. A lot of army kids come over here and never think of anything but the fun they're having. The girls are glad to have plenty of people to do the dusting and wash dishes and the boys don't have to mow the lawn or fire a furnace, so they whip around and have themselves a time. Tippy could have gone to Munich to school and could have had a date every night if she wanted to—but she didn't."

"No." Colonel Parrish sighed and shook his head. "What would you do?" he asked, blunt and persistent. "What would you do about Tippy if you thought you'd made a mistake? How would you straighten it out?"

"Why, sir," Ken tossed his cigarette in the fireplace and turned to lean on the arm of his chair, "I'd send her home," he answered, without hesitation. "If I were you, I'd send her back with Bobby."

"You would? Why?"

"Well, sir, I guess, for two reasons. One of them, we've talked about. Tippy needs to have her faith restored, and America can do it. That's what she needs. She's lost and she has to find herself."

"And the other reason?" Colonel Parrish's glance was keen and Ken raised his eyes to meet it.

"Me," he said.

There was a moment of silence while they both sought for words. The hiss and crackle of the fire was the only sound between them until Ken went on carefully, "I'm too fond of her, Colonel Parrish. But you needn't worry about it. I won't let her know it."

"Thank you, boy. I appreciate that."

"I didn't intend to come to Switzerland," he said, in a fine straightforward way. "But I'm not so old, either. I slip up and do things I know I haven't any business doing, like breaking down and coming here. But I don't think I've hurt Tippy. She likes me, sure; and that's as far as it goes. But you can't tell, it might grow into something. I'm the only male companion she has, and a lot of girls come over here, fall for some young officer and get married when they're only seventeen. One did it in Munich last week and her parents were sunk."

"I heard about that."

"So why shouldn't Tippy get to thinking I'm something, or want to get married because she's so lonely? I'm the only guy she sees."

Ken cut off his words. The muscles along his tense jaw rippled while Colonel Parrish considered him gravely. "You're a fine boy," the older man said with feeling. "I almost wish Tippy were twenty instead of such a difficult sixteen."

"You can bet I do, too, sir." Ken shot out a shy grin and said in a relieved tone, "But I'm glad you know how I feel. I want to play the game squarely, yet I don't want to get left out of the running."

"And I hope you won't be, son."

They smiled at each other in mutual understanding and liking, until Colonel Parrish remembered the original point of their conversation and slowly stated a fact to himself. "So," he said sighing, "you'd send her home if you were I."

"Yes, I guess I would. But there's one thing I'd like to ask you first and it's this, sir. Let me prepare her for it. Tip's apt to buck like a bronco over going, and well. . . ." He hesitated, then blurted out, "I think I can talk her into it better than you can. I can point things out to her better."

"Gladly." Tippy's father was ashamed to be shirking a duty but he clutched at the straw of rescue by adding, "I'll leave the field to you."

"It isn't a job I crave, since I don't want her to go, but I'll tackle it." Ken stood up and looked very boyish as he put his hands in his pockets, took them out again, and asked, "Do you think she could come back for a while next summer, just to visit? I'd get through the rest of the winter fine if I thought she might come back. And I'd be just as careful then," he promised, "as I'm being now."

"All right, boy. I think you've earned it and we'll work it out somehow."

"Then I'd better get on with my work. Tip's waiting for

me, and when you have something hard to do, it's best to plunge in and have it over."

"Thank you, Ken." Colonel Parrish stood up, too, and gratefully laid his hand on Kenneth Prescott's tweed sleeve. "When the time comes for me to help you," he added, with what comfort he could, "in a couple of years from now, you can bet I won't forget it."

"Gosh, sir! I'll count on that. Well. . . ." He took a backward step and ruefully ruffled up his unruly hair that, for once, lay flat. "If I get a chance to start talking, I'll report to you before dinner," he said, letting his hand come down in an informal salute. Then he plunged across the lounge and along the corridor to Tippy.

"Well, my goodness," she called, seeing him hesitate in the door, "the sandwiches are all curled up and your chocolate is stone cold. *Where* have you been?"

"I got hung up."

He pulled out a chair at the round table and sat down to face her. She tilted her head while she appraised him. "I like your blue sweater," she said, when he pitched into his hard dry sandwich as if he were starving.

"Um." He reached for the salt and was silently shaking it over white slabs of chicken, so she tried again, but reproachfully this time.

"People came and left, and I felt sort of silly sitting here. Even the accordion player thought it was no use to stay on just for me and went off to the cocktail lounge.

"I'm sorry, Tip."

"And the whipped cream fell down. Shall I order you another bowl of whipped cream?"

"No thanks."

And that was the end of that subject. Tippy was seldom at a loss for words with Ken and she rested her elbows on the table and cupped her chin in the palms of her hands. Her eyes were wide and troubled in her silence, and when he could swallow no more of the sandwich, he dropped a hard crust of bread back on his plate and slid his chair nearer hers.

"Tip," he said abruptly, knowing no other way to start, "I've been thinking a lot about the story Marga told one day. Can you remember what it was?"

"Do you mean about the little boy who lived in her block during the war—the little Jewish boy?"

"Yes, that's the one. What did she say about it?"

"Why, she said she had played with the little boy, and one day, when she was walking past his house with her grandmother, he was huddled on the steps, crying. Furniture was thrown all over the yard and the Nazis had killed his mother and father. Marga cried when she told it, and she said she tried to run to the little boy but her grandmother ran after her. Her grandmother told her, 'There isn't anything you can do for him, child, and we mustn't be caught here.' She never saw him again." It seemed a queer story to relate in the midst of a holiday, and she asked again, "Is that what you meant?"

"Yep, that's it." Ken nodded, and she went on sadly of her own accord:

"And Marga said that whenever she was naughty, the servants frightened her by saying 'You'd better behave yourself or you'll be sent to Dachau.' They didn't say 'Or I'll tell your mother,' as we do at home, they threatened her with Dachau. She didn't know what a terrible place it was because people were afraid even to talk about it, but she did know it was a prison." Tippy stopped and waited for some comment, wondering what had put Ken in this strange mood; and when he was silent, she asked anxiously, "What made you think about that?"

"I've been thinking how good America is. Nothing like that could happen over there."

"But, it has," she protested. "We made mistakes, too."

She said the words so positively that he stared at her. "What mistakes have we made?" he demanded.

[155]

"Well," Tippy decided that if he were going to be serious she might as well be, too, and she pushed away her plate and crossed her arms on the table. "We took land away from the Indians," she pointed out. "We crowded them back and back, and finally we gave them some territory we thought was worthless. It wasn't our idea for them to strike oil on it."

"Yes, I guess we did, at that." Ken was carefully leading her on and it was a great relief to have her walk so well alone, for she chronicled further:

"And we brought the Negroes over and sold them for slaves. We tore whole families apart as if they were cattle. Husbands and wives were dragged away from each other, and mothers never saw their children again. Those people were like the little Jewish boy; they loved their families. I've been worrying about it a lot lately. And while it all happened a long time ago, I don't see that America is so much better than Germany. We did the same thing."

"But a long time ago." He swung his chair farther around, leaned on the table and clasped the back of his head against his hand so that the two waving fronds of hair peeped through his fingers. "You see, Tip," he told her, "that's the important thing. We were a young country then and we made mistakes. Just like kids make more mistakes than grown-ups. And we had the enthusiasm of kids, too. We wanted to grow up to be a swell country and we never got tired, or discouraged, trying. And as we grew, we saw our mistakes and tried to fix 'em."

"Yes." Tippy nodded slowly. "I can see that," she acknowledged. "We're making the Negro a part of the American family, now, and trying to straighten things out, but. . . ." She stopped to shake her head, and he asked quickly:

"Doesn't that mean a lot? That, and the fact that we're trying to help the rest of the world get on its feet?"

"Golly, yes. I guess we are trying," she said with a sigh.

"Trying? My child, we're the greatest country on earth."

Ken dropped his hand and leaned across the table to her. "Do you know why we're a happy, successful nation of go-getters?" he asked. And he went on, without waiting for her answer, whatever it might be, "Take you, for example. You're lonesome. You haven't anything interesting to do, so you get down in the dumps, and the more you sit and think about it, the lower you sink. Suppose you're a whole country of people, German, Polish, Rumanian, any kind you want to name. You just think and think and talk to your neighbors about the rotten way life's going. But if you're an American, and lonesome, what do you do? Why, you clap on your hat and go to a movie. Or if you have to work, you run a vacuum cleaner or dump your laundry into a washing machine while you do the family chores and listen to the radio at the same time. People can't be as unhappy or full of unrest if they have something to take their mind off of their troubles. Anyone at home can buy a radio for five or six bucks. He can listen to people tell what they don't like about things and can put in his own word, too, if he wants to."

"And he can vote as he pleases."

"Sure. And he can go to the library and get a book on anything he wants to read. No one's going to tell him what he can read and what he can't."

"It is good." Tippy's smile shone out. "Ken," she cried, "I see what you mean! I don't know how we got on such a deep subject," she said, looking puzzled, "when I was feeling so silly and on top of the world, but it did clear up a lot of things that have been worrying me."

"I wish I were back there." The time had come. He had filled Tippy with nostalgia for America and now was the time to give her a gentle push toward it. "Three years is a long time to be away," he said sadly.

"Do you have to stay three years?"

"Yep. You only have to stay two because your father's due

to retire. But me? Well," he leaned back and rubbed his hot nervous palms on his knees, "I guess I'll spend my time in Heidelberg," he said.

"Why Heidelberg instead of Munich?"

She came forward with her problem just as he had moved away with his, and he felt a prick of conscience for stating a fact which, as yet, was only a possibility. The transfer to Heidelberg was his to accept or reject. Yesterday, in spite of knowing it to be more interesting work, he had decided to stay close to Garmisch. Now. . . . His little talk with Colonel Parrish had pointed the way as definitely as any sign post, and he decided reluctantly, "I'm going there, Tip."

"When?"

"Quite soon, I think. They've offered me a job in G-3."

"Oh." Tippy dropped back, too. She tried to smile, to wish him luck, but no words came out. She could only think of how lonely she would be.

"I won't get down very often," he went on, reading her mind. "I wish you knew more people, Tip. Or better still, I wish you were back home with a gang your age. You should be going to dances up at the Point and playing juke boxes in drug stores, eating pop corn in the movies and whipping around in cars. This is no life for a girl."

Tippy looked thoughtful. Garmisch without Ken, she groaned inwardly. Days and days of loneliness like the ones she had borne at first. And then her thoughts turned to the Germans there. She was helping them, a little, and perhaps she should forget about herself and go on; and she sat with her eyes on the empty chocolate cups and knew that two tears were about to spill out.

But Ken's voice penetrated her misery. "You know, Tip," it said in the light conversational tone he had suddenly adopted, "what I think would be swell?"

"Wh-what?"

"For you to go home and finish your school and then come

[158]

back again next summer. I could get a whole month's leave then, and could come down to Garmisch before you go back to college."

Tippy reached up and ran the tip of her finger along her wet lashes. There was nothing else to do. The drops were growing larger and larger and she had to blink to make them stay back. "It would be—fun," she sighed. "I. . . ." Then she stopped.

"And I think your folks would like it. Your Dad's pretty worried because he thinks they've made a mess of your life but he doesn't know how to undo it. That's why I was late coming in. We got to talking about you."

"Oh. You did?"

"Sure. I kind of got the idea that he'd be awfully pleased if you'd ask to go back home for the rest of the winter. Just from little things he said," Ken added. "And I'll hate going off to Heidelberg and worrying about you. Perhaps I'd better turn it down."

"Oh, no!" Tippy's startled hand flew to her throat. She had been in the army long enough to know that officers must never let women stand in their way of advancement. "You can't do that!" she cried. "If the job's a good one, you have to take it." Her tears crept back into their ducts again, leaving her eyes bright with entreaty. "I'd feel awful if I thought you gave up anything just to help me."

"Well, you think things over. If your father should pop the question to you, you'll have had a little warning and will know that the United States is a darned good place to be." He pushed back his chair and said casually, just as if he hadn't shaken her world to pieces, "How about hunting up that accordion guy and dancing?"

"All right."

He laid some francs on the table and was conscious that she got up and turned away. He had dealt them each a blow, he thought sadly. Or what was even worse, he had picked a bud from its nest of green leaves before ever it had a chance to flower. "What a fool I am," he muttered, wishing he could link his arm through hers, could say, "Cherub, I didn't mean it. No matter what they say, *I* need you here."

But she was already walking to the door. And when he crossed the lounge beside her, he saw Colonel Parrish still sitting in his chair and sent him a final, affirmative nod.

CHAPTER XIII

"So THAT's the way it is," Tippy told Alice, taking off her white wool dress and folding it to pack. "They bring me here, they send me home. And all three of them, including Ken, are as casual about it as if I were playing on a see-saw. Ups-a-daisy, downs-a-daisy, isn't it fun, Tippy?"

"How do you feel about it?" Alice stopped her own packing and stood with a bottle of shampoo soap in her hand while she waited for an answer. When none came, she sat down on the bed and tried again, "Do you want to stay or go home?"

"I don't care." Tippy shrugged. "It doesn't seem to make much difference, one way or the other. I didn't want to come, certainly, but I got here and hung on by my teeth. I'm getting kind of used to it, now," she said, yawning. "Anyone's an idiot who wouldn't want to live in the States, but I had some sort of idea that I could do my bit toward making this a better place and could promote democracy. I've tried," she ended. "Goodness knows, I've tried."

She picked up a pair of shoes while Alice sat in silence, wrapped them in a soiled slip and tucked them neatly in the end of the case. "I always seem to be packing to go somewhere," she said with a wry chuckle, as if the idea were funny. "Next stop America."

"Oh, Tip, you're just mad." Alice twisted around and looked over the bed's high, old fashioned footboard. "Look," she pointed out from a confused certainty in her own mind, "You know your mother and father are right about this. They're worried because you aren't having the right kind of school, or friends, or anything. If you had a child you'd feel the same way about her, but *you* don't want to be told what to do."

"Maybe." Tippy dropped the lid of her case and her lips were tight. She walked across the room to the dresser and stood, separating the collection of jars and bottles on it. "This is my stuff," she said. "You can have what's left."

"Tip. . . ."

"What?"

"Aren't you mad?"

There was no chance to evade. Alice would bore into her, would probe and ask questions until she answered, so she left her share of make-up in its cluster and slipped on her warm robe. "Yes, I guess you might say I'm mad," she returned wearily, flinging herself on the desk chair.

"But why? When you know it's right?"

It was hard to put into words. Why was she angry? Tippy wondered. She had felt only sad when Ken had told her that her parents wanted her to go home, unhappily sad; and, later, secretly glad. America had reached out and claimed her. Her old life would be hers again, the full, rich life with not enough hours in the day to hold it. No ruins and desolation to look at. No fantastic dragon to trouble her dreams, no little man of the mountains who proclaimed that indestructible Nature provided the only peace. She would be away from it all and could push it back into the limbo of forgotten things. So where had sadness changed to anger?

"I don't know, Alcie," she said slowly. "I just feel that, somewhere along the way, I'm being cheated. All my life, people have been building up my ideals and a fine moral code. I even had to be taught to be kind, because when I was too little to remember it, I wouldn't let a little girl ride on my sled. She was poor and didn't have one, and I pushed her off of mine. We were visiting at Gran's then, and Mums took us down to a hardware store and bought her a new sled; and she talked to me about sharing with children who didn't have as much as I had. And I was taught to be honest, and do my lessons the best I could, and to stick to things that were hard. Why, even last year, when I thought I had grown up enough to be called Miss Tippy, Trudy said I had to wait and earn the title."

"Yes, I remember that." Alice folded her arms along the foot of the bed and rested her chin on them. "But what does all that have to do with your being mad about going home?" she asked, trying not to let Tippy see how sleepy she was. "You can go on developing a good character at home."

"Yes, I know that, but . . . oh, gosh, don't you see? All these years while I was being 'developed,' as you call it, I was only learning the stuff they taught me. Now they don't want me to use it. It's just as if they said, 'Don't be kind, don't do the best you can, don't help people. Go home and have fun.' And that's not fair."

"Maybe not." Alice was so tired her eyes refused to stay open any longer, and she knew the hours until morning were ticking away inexorably. But she had to make sure Tippy understood that her parents were doing what seemed best and right to them, so she said patiently, "Sometimes a man has a job and he works hard at it, but it just isn't any good. Maybe he isn't fitted for it, or—well, anyway, it isn't the right job for him. And someone says, 'Hey, I've got a better one for you.' Don't you think he'd be a dope not to take it?"

"Sure, if he knows it's better. But how would he know?"

"Because it's the kind of work he's done before—before he got out of that line of work and into a new one. It has some chance for advancement in it."

Tippy conceded the point. "Yes, I see that," she acknowledged. "At least, I see what you see, but it doesn't stop me from feeling I got a raw deal. I wasn't offered a better job. I got fired."

"Well, anyway, you're coming home. Oh, Tip!" Alice scrambled up off the bed and stretched both arms above her head. "I've felt so awful about leaving tomorrow," she said, yawning openly now. "But, it's all right. We'll have fun, and, oh boy, won't Peter be glad!"

"I hope someone will."

Tippy got up to find her pajamas, discovered she had packed them, and opened her case again. "Well, good night," she said resignedly, looking at her roommate who was already a mound under the covers. "I'll see you around the last of January at a West Point hop." Then she morosely trailed her pajamas into the bathroom.

Morning came in a flash, and Tippy's gloomy thoughts returned with it. This might very well be her last glimpse of Ken—one brief farewell in the lobby; and wanting to have it alone, she left Alice to cope with the luggage, and went downstairs. But Bobby greeted her as she stepped out of the elevator.

"Well, what do you know!" he said. "Mums and Dad have had breakfast and have gone down to see about the cars, and Ken has something he says he wants to show you."

"Where is he?"

"Search me. He's been romping back and forth through here, and the last time he galloped past me he said for you to meet him. . . ." Bobby stopped, frowned, and trying to be more explicit, covered the world in general with a sweep of his hand. "I don't know," he gave up. "I never saw a guy point in so many directions at once. Outdoors, I guess. At least, he ended up going that way."

"Well, for goodness' sake." Tippy banged through the door, and after looking up and down the empty driveway, asked a porter who was guarding the growing line of luggage, "Have you seen a young man go by?"

But he shook his head. "No man," he answered. She stood indecisively on the hard cold snow until he volunteered a question of his own. "You look for ze sleigh, yes?"

"Perhaps. But not till later."

"A man comes. He is a old man and is behind ze hotel. Your young man, is zere, too, I zink."

"Oh, thank you. *Merci.*"

Tippy wished for her galoshes as she picked her way over a frozen waste of ruts and around the long building. Switzerland was a pleasant place in warm clothes but not in open-toed sandals and a fur coat without buttons. A steady whistling wind blew her off her course, and as she pushed on, she told herself, "I really should go back. I could see whatever he has to show me from inside. It's crazy to follow him clear out here."

The air was crisp and cold, and she took it into her lungs in long refreshing breaths; and as the sheltered side of the hotel was not as windy, she managed to reach the back where stables and a kitchen wing made a snug courtyard. A red sleigh was drawn up in the enclosure, and Ken, back in his uniform and trenchcoat, was standing beside it with a burly farmer. "Yoo-hoo," she called, just as he leaned over to look inside the sleigh again.

"Hey. Good morning," he turned and shouted in answer. "Come here and see what I've found."

Tippy skidded over the snow, not minding cold balls that squeezed under the toes of her thin stockings, and when she slid to a stop, he pushed her in front of him.

Three black, woolly puppies looked at her from the back seat of the sleigh. They stood in a row and stared with their beady black eyes, their stumps of tails wagging like quivering harp strings.

"Rovers!" she cried, jumping up and squeezing in beside them. "Oh, the blessed, cute, darlings. Oh, Ken, how did you find them?"

"I was asking around, and one of the porters told me a family here owned some," he answered. "And they sent them in with their chauffeur, or whatever you call him. He says the fellow next to you has the best points. Do you like him?"

"Oh, *yes!*" Tippy reached down for the puppy, but the one on the end climbed over his brothers and onto her lap. He stood up and licked her face and gave a short joyful bark that was little more than a squeak and managed to wriggle inside her coat. "They're all so darling," she said, trying to hold him still and look at his less energetic family at the same time." But he stiffened his small back, flung both paws against her chest and covered her face with kisses.

He was one bouncing mass of wool and enthusiasm, and she stopped trying to see over his head or through him. "He's mine," she decided, without delay, cuddling him closer. "I guess we've just chosen each other."

Ken grinned and patted the puppy, the wagging rear end, which was all he could reach, and he seconded her choice by saying, "That's swell. I've had a leaning toward the little fellow, too. He's so darned engaging and knows what he wants."

"He's darling." Tippy wanted to pet the two that would ride home again in the sleigh, but the bundle in her arms loved her too much. He whimpered, he kissed her, he pressed his round puppy stomach against her chest and danced his joy; and at last she had to pass him to Ken and climb down. "Perhaps it's better if I don't get fond of the others," she said, reaching for hers again when he tried to leap through space to her. "I might want them all."

"It's all right, because you couldn't have them, anyway. The people really want to keep one of them and they have a place for whichever one's left over. I have a hunch that this is the one they liked and wanted to keep because our friend over there kept trying to push the other two at me. All settled?"

"All settled! Oh, Ken, I'm so grateful." The puppy, now that his future was secure, was seized with excited trembling, and she carefully tucked him under her coat. "Do I . . . the man. . . ." she stammered, but Ken grinned at her and answered:

"He's a delayed Christmas present. I didn't think I'd ever find him and I never was satisfied with giving you just a bunch of books. Come on. The mercenary end of the deal's been closed and we'd better all get in where it's warm."

Tippy tried to let the puppy say good-by to his brothers, but he had lost interest in them. He was so sleepily snuggled against her that she nodded gratefully to the driver of the sleigh and let Ken lead her into a kitchen entrance and through a back corridor of the hotel.

"What do you think you'll name him?" he asked, when they were inside where it was warm. "His mother's Swiss and his father's Belgian and he has plenty of ancestors. I have his birth certificate in my pocket and you might pick out a string of names from it."

"I think I'll just call him Switzy," she said promptly, looking up. "I got him in Switzerland, and I knew a dog named Fritzy, once. Switzy isn't much funnier, is it? Do you think?"

"Switzy's a swell name. Hi, Switz, old boy." Ken ruffled the contented puppy's fuzzy topknot, and she asked with a worried frown:

"What will I do about him when I have to go home? I can't go off and leave him."

"That's all taken care of, too," he assured her airily, stopping in the head porter's cubbyhole before he opened a door to the main lounge. "I have a couple of classmates who are always flying to the States and back. They'll deliver Mr. Switz right to Mitchell Field and all you'll have to do is have a car there to meet him."

"I'll borrow David's limousine," she laughed bending down to kiss the cold damp nose so close to her chin. "Mr. Switz deserves at least a limousine or an official car."

"And we'll stop and buy him a collar in St. Gallen."

"St. Gallen? Are you going home that way, too?" Tippy's head jerked up and he returned, with a smug, important look:

"I am. Do you think your mother and father would want to ride along with a dog?"

"Well, wonder of wonders!" she chuckled happily, and he went on:

"We'll be four in my car until Jenifer picks up Alcie at some little town they decided on last night. Five," he corrected, "counting our new passenger here."

"All I can say is, you've been mighty busy this morning."

"That's me."

Ken opened the door for her and when they were inside the large, safe lounge, she put the puppy down on his four short legs. He bounced and frisked and spun in circles. And seeing a small black cyclone chasing itself, Bobby and Alice jumped up from a divan where they had been patiently waiting.

"He's mine," Tippy said proudly, patting her chest. "Ken gave him to me. Meet Mr. Switzy."

"Well, for the love of. . . ." Bobby looked down at the puppy. It had finished an excursion that covered a radius of twenty feet or less, and was expressing its joy at finding Tippy again; and he asked disgustedly, "Is that one of those things that wears puffs and pompoms?"

"Not Switzy. He's going to be a poodle in the rough. In summer he's going to look like a little black lamb, and in winter he'll wear a fur coat and chaps. He'll be a hand-clipped job like Rover, won't you darling?" She caught up her adoring admirer and Bobby growled through pangs of hunger:

"What are you planning to do with him while we have breakfast? It's time, now, to meet Mums and Dad."

"He'll sit on my lap." She tucked the puppy under her arm, and following her into the dining room, Alice giggled and pointed to Tippy's leopard sleeve that had sprouted a sausage tail.

And Switzy was the happiest one on the trip back to Garmisch. When Alice left the car for a train along the way, he kissed her good-by with great affection. He kissed her pretty

[168]

sister, too, and untied the shoe lace of the future Earl of Easterbrook.

"I'll see you soon, Alcie," Tippy whispered, feeling no loss in parting because she was eager to get home with her new charge. "Tell Peter I'll write to him as soon as I can and I'll come up to a hop. And kiss Donny and Bitsy for me."

"You won't get upset again about leaving?"

"No, Switzy and I'll make out. They even have better shots for distemper in America, and he can eat dog biscuits while I have a chocolate soda, so he'll be happy."

Tippy's face wore a different look from its sad expression of the night before, and Alice gave a sigh of relief. "All right," she said, backing reluctantly away. "Your father wants to go on. I'll see you."

"Soon." Tippy scooped up her puppy and ran to Ken's car. "Alcie's a darling," she said, settling down on the front seat and not minding how glum Bobby was, behind her. "Just think how awful I acted about coming on this trip, and what a wonderful time I've had. It was the most perfect time I've ever known."

"You always say that." Ken gave her an amused grin and she held Switzy up to kiss him.

"Ugh," Bobby said from the back. Then he stretched his legs across the seat and disgustedly settled down for a nap.

CHAPTER XIV

SWITZY liked going for walks. Wearing a fine red collar, he had trotted all over Garmisch and was a personal friend of Rover's. He kept Tippy so busy that she hurried through her lessons and was off and far away before Mrs. Parrish could ask, "Darling, what have you done with your green skirt?" or "Where did you put those wash dresses you brought over?"

Tippy knew her mother was getting the clothes ready to pack, for there had been so many family conferences. Bobby had left on a plane and she was going by transport.

"We'll all feel better about it that way," Colonel Parrish had decided the night after their return from Switzerland, when they sat in a family group. "Bob hasn't much gear to pack and we can put him on a train for Paris, the day after tomorrow. But it's too sudden just to be shoving Tippy off. She isn't ready. We aren't either," he added with a sigh.

Tippy was sitting on the floor, playing with her puppy, and she went on rolling a ball for him. She had agreed to any suggestions they made: to go, to delay, to fly or sail, and when her mother asked reluctantly, "Doesn't it matter to you, dear, which you do?" she shook her head.

"Fetch, Switz!" she ordered, catching the puppy up and hugging him when he accidentally obeyed her and dropped the ball in her lap. "Isn't he cute?"

"Yes, but you'll have to pay some attention to us," her mother protested.

"Huh?" Tippy looked up then, her face a blank. "Oh, anything you decide's all right," she said, and rolled the ball again.

So, with a despairing shrug, her father telephoned Colonel Jackson in Bremerhaven, and she was going home under the protecting wing of mutual friends from Frankfurt.

"Just think, Tip, you'll be there when Penny's new baby comes," her mother said wistfully, one morning, when Tippy's sailing date was definitely decided. "And you can stay with Alcie while Bobby takes his West Point examinations on the Island. You'll know right away if he passes his physical."

"Oh, he'll pass. I'll send you a cable to tell you he did." Tippy was setting out her lesson books for Mrs. Tremaine, and she asked politely, "Why don't you come with me?"

"I can't," Mrs. Parrish sighed. "I have to stay with Dad."

Sure. You stick to your job. Tippy thought the words but hadn't the courage to mutter them aloud, and she listened to her mother say:

"I saw Annie in that blue polka dot of yours last night. You did give it to her, didn't you?"

"Umhum. She went to a party at some German's house. I helped her bake a cake for it, too. We followed the recipe on the box and it turned out all right."

"But why, honey? I don't mean the cake, but why do you keep on giving away everything you own?"

"The stores have plenty of clothes in America."

"But we haven't plenty of money."

"Then, I'll wear what I have or borrow from Penny." Tippy was casual as she slid carefully along her bench and tried not to wake Switzy who had fallen asleep on the cushion. And she said with a slow smile, "You'd better run along about your business or Mrs. Tremaine will find me dumber than usual this morning."

So Mrs. Parrish had given up and left.

"Tippy isn't like herself," she worried to her husband, that evening when they were alone in their room. "She used to be so silly and noisy; but all through Bobby's last few days she didn't even fight with him. I used to think she was as effervescent and effusive as Penny, but sometimes she makes me think of David."

"Why David?" he asked with a frown.

"Because David was often a grave, thoughtful child. He felt things more deeply than Penny. Oh, perhaps he didn't feel them more deeply, but he showed his feelings less. He worked things out within himself, quietly and carefully. Trudy always said that David walked straight. Even as a little thing, he knew where he was going and went there."

"Well, is that so bad?" he asked, smiling, and trying to comfort her.

"No, not for David," she answered. "But he was a boy. You don't expect boys to confide their thoughts and feelings to you. I don't know what Tippy's thinking," she sighed. "I don't even know if she wants to go home, or if she's happy over it, or unhappy, or what." She shook her head helplessly, and Colonel Parrish asked:

"What does she say? Doesn't she talk about it when you're packing her stuff?"

"No. Not any more than you've heard her say. She brings me things when I ask for them, if she still has them, that is, and says 'all right' to anything I mention. Then she slides out with her dog."

"Where does she go?"

"That, I don't know, either. Sometimes she goes to the Vanderhoefs. I do know that much because she always comes in happier and tells me silly little things about Rover and Switzy. She. . . ." Mrs. Parrish hesitated, then stopped and asked suddenly, "You don't think she's got too serious over Ken, do you?"

"No. He says she hasn't, and the guy ought to know. I knew how you felt about me," he bragged, hoping to tease her into a smile; but she only suggested:

"Let's ask him to drive down one evening. Perhaps he can dig something out of her that we can't reach. I hate to call in outside help for one of my own children, but this has me baffled. I thought sending her home would throw her into swirls of joy, but it hasn't. All her life Tippy's been everything under the shining sun but quiet," she worried. "Now it's as if her very thoughts move on tip-toe."

"That's a nice metaphor, or whatever you call 'em." Colonel Parrish lighted a cigarette and sat staring at it. "I hate to ask Ken," he said at last. "The boy has his problem, too, and he's trying to handle it in a way that's best for Tip and all of us. He expects to come down next week-end and tell her good-by. Can't we wait till then and see what happens?"

"But she'll leave on Tuesday, and *nothing* will happen. If only I had Penny here she could take care of it. I might ask Jeannie Vanderhoef to. . . ." Mrs. Parrish broke off the sentence and opened her door and crossed the hall.

Tippy was sitting on her bed in her pajamas, tying a red ribbon in a bunch of curly fuzz on Switzy's forehead and she looked up with a laugh. "Doesn't he look ridiculous?" she cried, pinching the ribbon to make it stand up out of his sight. "And isn't he vain?" she added, when the puppy cocked his head in his clownish way.

"He's a sweet little fellow, and I'll miss you both when you're gone." Mrs. Parrish sat down on the bed, too, ready to begin one of her hopeless conversations, but Tippy only said casually:

"Oh, you'll be home soon. Look, he's learned a new trick." And she bent over to put the little dog on the floor. "Sit up, Switzy," she coaxed. "Stiffen your backbone. There. Isn't that good?"

"He really ought to be in a circus," Mrs. Parrish laughed, trying to be gay and match Tippy's mood, wishing she knew as much about her child as Switzy did. And she said without thinking, "I wish he could talk."

[173]

"I do, too." Tippy stayed bent over and looking down at the puppy who had dropped to all fours and sat regarding her adoringly. "He does, sometimes, though, and he's an awfully good listener."

"What does he listen to?"

"Oh. . . ." She swung around to sit cross-legged, pulling Switzy up beside her. "I tell him about all the things we're going to do," she said. For one flash of a second her face was alive, then it closed again. "It's kind of dumb, talking to a dog, isn't it?"

"Not if you haven't anyone else to talk to."

"Well, I will have when I get home." Tippy pushed back in the bed and yawned. "It's awfully late, Mums," she said. "Aren't we keeping Dad awake?"

"I don't think so, honey. Well, perhaps we are." Mrs. Parrish stood up meekly, and Tippy bounced out to put her puppy on his pallet.

"Good night, Mums, darling," she said, straightening and reaching out both arms. "I love you such a lot."

"I love you, too, my precious."

"I—I'm awfully grumpy sometimes, Mums, but you don't mind it, do you?"

"No, darling, I don't mind." Mrs. Parrish held her breath, afraid to take the lead, afraid to spoil whatever confidences Tippy might decide to offer, but she only received another hug and the careless:

"Then that's all right. I'll turn out the lamp if you can see your way through the hall."

"I'll turn it out. Good night."

" 'Night." Tippy climbed back into bed again; and when the room was dark, Switzy padded across the floor and put both front paws on the covers. "You should be asleep," she told him, lying still and stroking him gently. "Little dogs who don't have problems should go to sleep."

But Switzy had a problem. He wanted to be in bed with

Tippy and he couldn't jump that high. He clutched and pawed at the covers until she got up and carried him back to his pallet. Then she turned on the lamp, put on her robe, and sat down at her desk.

For a long time she just sat there, her bare feet hooked over the rungs of her chair, her arm propped on the desk, her hand holding her forehead. Then, without changing position she pulled some stationery from a drawer and began to write a letter.

The words flowed along without effort and she seldom stopped to consider what she should put down. At last, however, when several sheets were covered, she held her pen in her teeth while she sorted the pages, and with her arms crossed on her knees, bent over to scan them.

"Peter dear:" (she read)

"I haven't written you a decent letter in ages, but I've been so terribly muddled. I think I simply forgot about the way you used to understand things, the kind, nice way you had of figuring things out, and of being—well, it sounds silly to say it, but being helpful. Goodness knows, I've needed help ever since I got here. I've thought— Oh, Peter, I just have to talk to you about something, and will you please cable back if you think I'm right? Not that you have to make my decision—it's made—but just to give me your opinion. You're not much older than I am and we don't always think like older people do.

"Everyone says I should come home. I know they're worrying about what is best for me. But you see, what they don't understand is. . . ."

She heard a noise in the hall and turned her head.

"Tippy?" Her mother's voice called softly. "Are you still up?"

[175]

"Yes, I was writing a letter." She opened the desk drawer and swiftly crammed the pages into it, just as Mrs. Parrish appeared in the door. "I'm through, though, now," she said.

"Then, hop into bed, child. It's as cold as a snowdrift in here. Why, honey," Mrs. Parrish's anxious voice ended in a shiver and asked, "Didn't you know the window was open?"

"I didn't feel cold." She laid Switzy's blanket over him then slid under her own covers. "You scoot back," she urged, "before you freeze."

"Is anything troubling you, dear?"

Her mother still hesitated and Tippy shook her head. "Not a thing," she answered. "I swear it, Scout's honor. I'm as happy as a June bug."

"Oh, honey, I wish I were sure. . . ."

"Well, you can be. Now, Mums," Tippy scolded, "Go, get in bed. I'll tell you I am, tomorrow. Truly, I will. I'll tell you at," she looked at the small traveling clock beside her bed, and promised, "at five o'clock when Dad comes home. I'll tell you I'm happy. Will that satisfy you?"

"Why then? We thought we'd invite Ken down tomorrow or the next day—and—and have a little dinner for you," she finished lamely.

"Then I'll tell him, too. I'll tell the whole world, but, please, go back where it's warm."

"All right, honey. I will."

Mrs. Parrish padded away for the second time and Tippy lay wondering where her parents would find enough people to invite to a party. She thought of getting up again to read the rest of her letter, then decided it really was cold, so snuggled down.

A great load seemed to have rolled off her chest. It was as if she had been pinned down by a stone until, after a long nightmarish struggle she had managed to push the stone off; or as if she had been trapped in a dark room with something frightening penned in with her, something that listened for her to breathe and was ready to spring. Only on her long walks with Switzy had she found any peace. She could talk to Switzy, and whatever she said was right. Every troubled thought brought on a wag of his stubby tail. He agreed with her anger, pitied her indecision, and approved her sudden determination. His talkative tail told her so. It fanned her loneliness straight into oblivion.

"Good little Switzy," she whispered, and, for the first time in days, felt no dread of tomorrow.

Colonel Parrish had gone when she came down to break-fast, for she was purposely late. Her mother was trying to make a party list out of nothing but a pencil, a sheet of paper and a telephone directory; and Tippy was relieved to see Mrs. Tremaine peddling up the driveway. "I can't help you now," she called, speeding for the sunroom. "Why don't you skip it?"

"Because we want to have some sort of farewell for you," her mother repeated with grim determination, padding along behind. "What about. . . ." But Tippy interrupted:

"There isn't anyone I'd want to have but the Vanderhoefs, and perhaps that cute little bride I met, who's only eighteen. She and her husband seem kind of bewildered about life in Garmisch, so you might ask them." She flung her books on the table and mumbled while she sorted out papers, "And you might ask Inge and Robert, or else that silly Kay Macklin and her current love. I suppose it would have to be one or the other, because Kay's so high-toned and fancy. Now, scoot."

Mrs. Parrish fled, and Tippy plunged into her morning's work.

I have until five o'clock, she thought, when she should have been writing a French translation. "I'll walk out to Head-quarters and mail my letter to Peter, and I can rehearse all the things I'm going to say to Mums and Dad along the way."

But just before noon Mrs. Tremaine developed a sick head-ache. Her healthy pink cheeks turned unexpectedly pale, and

Tippy had to roll her bicycle into the garage and drive her home in the car. And when Tippy returned, Colonel Parrish's official car was parked in the driveway.

"This is it," she muttered with a sigh. "And I'm really not ready. Oh, my soul!"

She had the same frightened feeling that had often attacked her in America when an unexpected examination was thrust at her by a teacher, and she sidled into the house as if it were a classroom. She could hear her mother and father talking in the living room and she tried to keep Switzy quiet as she slipped out of her coat. But her mother heard her and called:

"Tippy? Come here a minute, darling."

"In just a second." She opened the basement door and thrust the puppy through. "Go on, get your milk," she ordered, shutting him in and not waiting to see if he sat on the step and howled or obeyed her. Then she took the long march in full view of her parents and stopped in the last doorway.

"We have the party all arranged," Mrs. Parrish said, gayly. "Tonight's officers' night at the Casa, so we thought we'd have everyone here to dinner, then reserve a table for you. Ken can come if he drives back tonight, and the Vanderhoefs are. . . ."

"Wait a minute." Tippy pulled down her sweater and stood with her hands clamped to its hem. "You may not want to give a farewell bust when you hear what I have to say," she told her. "I'm not going home."

"You're not *what?*" Mrs. Parrish dropped the scratch pad she was holding out, and with it lying on the floor between them like a white flag, Tippy's eyes went down to it, then up again.

"I said I'd tell you this afternoon why I'm suddenly happy," she answered clearly, quite calm now and seeing her way. "I wanted time to—to . . . well, it doesn't make much difference. I've made up my mind, and I don't want to go home."

"But, Tip, why not?" Her father asked, looking at her with a puzzled frown. "We've thought you weren't happy here."

"I know you did." Tippy pulled the desk chair over to face him and sat sideways on it. "Listen," she said, hooking her arm over its back, "I haven't been what you'd call bursting with joy, but hiking back home wouldn't be any better. Now, wait a minute, Dad," she begged, when he tried to speak. "For one thing, I'd have to go out and stay with Penny. That would be fine for me, but do you think it's fair to Penny and Josh?" Her father's perplexed eyes clouded, and she saw she had made a point. "You know it isn't," she told him, shaking her head. "Josh married Penny, not her sister, too, and they don't want a gang of teen-agers cluttering up their house or to have to wait up till I get home, like you and Mums do. They'll get all that, someday, with Parri, and they'd just be taking over a responsibility that belongs to us. You can't be unfair to one child just because another one doesn't like the spot she's in, can you?"

"No." Colonel Parrish agreed reluctantly, and she hurried on:

"Well, that's one of the biggest reasons why I'm not going, but it isn't the only one. I have lots of others."

"What are they, darling?" her mother asked, studying Tippy with growing wonder, while she listened to her say:

"I've been angry. I told Alcie I was mad, because I didn't think you were fair to me. You just moved me around like a —a pawn in a chess game, or a baby, or something. But that didn't matter so much, because people have to decide for their children and guide them. The point was, you didn't seem to think I had any stamina. You didn't respect me."

"Why, honey. . . ."

"I know, Dad." Tippy turned her eyes back to her father

[179]

and said in a more comforting tone, "You love me so much that you think I always have to be happy. Of course, I'd like to be, but—people can't. Not real people, who think and feel. I'd like to go back and eat hot dogs and dance and have fun. Who wouldn't? But I love you and Mums, too. I'd be lonesome for you over there, just the way I'm lonesome for America over here. I'd still be all torn apart. I've *been* torn apart," she said, "just thinking about it."

"I know, child," he sighed. "We have, too."

"Then what good would it do?" Tippy dropped her arm and leaned forward with both hands on the chair seat. "Don't you see, Dad?" she said earnestly. "You can't make a person happy by poking some sort of substitute at him, any more than you can cure a child who's sick by giving it a toy. I'm the fellow who has to decide what's going to make me well. Running away and barging in on Penny won't do it. I've been a pretty weak character ever since I cried on her at the dock, and I admit I've been a trial over here. I've tried not to be, but. . . ." She shook her head slowly and said above their protests, "I had to get used to things. I had to find out for myself the things I've been telling you. Penny might have seen them quicker than I did, or not minded about them, and I know Bobby would have pushed them around and made everything just fine for himself. But I couldn't. I'm not like they are," she ended. "I guess I'm—just me."

"Thank goodness for that." Colonel Parrish considered her with obvious respect and affection, then turned to his wife. "One of our best?" he asked, with a lift of his eyebrows and looking proud when she nodded.

"Oh, Tippy, darling," she cried, getting up and lovingly smoothing back her child's bright hair. "You make Dad and me so proud of you. Not because you want to stay," she explained quickly, pressing Tippy's head against her. "That decision is up to you and we'll do whatever you want about it; but because you're such a loving, considerate child."

"Thank you, Mums." Tippy reached up and locked her arms around her mother's waist. "Do you truly want me to stay?" she asked, looking up.

"You know we do, darling. We thought we'd just die over sending you off. But we've tried to consider your future."

"I know you have, and I have, too." Tippy nuzzled her cheek against Mrs. Parrish's belt and said carefully, "I know I have to have an education and can't mope around like a ghost in the house, so I thought if you didn't mind—that I'd take a whack at going to Munich to school. If the Germans can stand it to live in that mess, I certainly can stand it to look at them. And I'd make friends there," she explained. "I'd only have to be away four nights at a time and I could ask Martha McCallister down here to visit and could go and see her. I might even get kind of crazy about it and hate to go back home to college," she said with a chuckle.

"Oh, you might, honey, or we might go home with you," her mother added, kissing the top of her head. "We never know what's in the future, you know." And she bent down to whisper loudly, "We might try and coax Dad to retire."

"Well, perhaps you could." Colonel Parrish had heard the words intended for him, and looked as well pleased as the two before him. He was about to be more explicit when he saw Jochen speeding through the hall toward the sunroom, his tin tray covered with rattling luncheon dishes. "We can go on with our talk at lunch," he said from necessity. "But, I vote to have a party tonight, anyway. We can call it a welcome home bust."

CHAPTER XV

KEN covered the seventy-five miles to Garmisch in record time. He dreaded to think of what he might find there, for Mrs. Parrish's voice had been almost incoherent on the telephone, and had left him with some idea that Tippy's farewell party was being given because she was leaving suddenly, tomorrow. But when he spun gravel and stopped at the door, Tippy clopped across the lawn on her skis and called to him through the early dusk.

"Hey, what's the rush?" she asked, sliding her shoes out of the straps and walking the rest of the way on foot. "Going to a fire, friend?"

"I was trying to beat your dinner guests here," he said, sliding out on the snow beside her, "because I wanted to talk to you. Am I early enough?"

"I haven't even thought about dressing, yet," she laughed. "Jeannie and I've been skiing up back of the house and she just went home, too. I have to go to the restaurant and pick up the ice cream Mums ordered," she added, "so how about driving me?"

"Hop in."

Ken opened the door for her and she sat down with her snowy boots firmly planted on the rubber mat. "I'm tired," she said, pulling off her mittens and resting her hands on her knees. "I didn't learn as much in Switzerland as I thought I did and Jeannie and I are a couple of crazies together. Especially with Craig and Rover and Switzy in the middle of things. We had fun, though." She leaned back against the seat and looked at him. "How are you?" she asked.

"I'm fine. But what's all this about you hopping off so suddenly?" Ken swung the car along the road and she grinned at him.

"I'm not hopping off," she said. "In fact, I'm not going anywhere at all. I'm staying."

"Right here in Garmisch, you mean? For Pete's sake, why?"

He risked a look at her and she braced herself against the door as they struck a bump. She smiled at him with her eyes, but her lips were serious as she answered calmly, "I thought things out, Ken. It's all a long story that covers about a week of muddling around in my mind, but, as I told Dad and Mums today, I want to see things through. I want to go to school in Munich and make friends over here. That's the part I told *them,* at least, but I guess you know the other things I want to do, don't you?"

"Such as killing that dragon?" He regarded her humorously and she nodded.

"I don't have to kill him," she said. "All I have to do is show people that he's already dead. He's just a bunch of make-believe, and if everyone could know that—a lot of the people at home, too, who go around shouting that the country's in a terrible state—the world would be wonderful. It would be as fine as your little man of the mountain thinks Nature is."

They rattled over a bridge and Ken remembered their other conversation at this same spot, and asked, "Just what have you decided the dragon to be, Tip?"

"Oh. . . ." She stopped and thought for a moment, before she went on, "I still haven't tried to put him into words exactly, but you might say he's a scary old thing that has skin made out of tyranny. His bony structure is hard, cold, greed, and the Europeans have always thought, and I guess they still think it, that the fire he snorts out, is power. Gosh," she said disgustedly, "he can't breathe enough fire to light a candle."

[183]

"Tippy Parrish, you're a riot." Ken stopped the car in front of the Post Exchange restaurant and threw back his head in a shout. "You're really—something," he said, when he could look at her again.

"Why?" Tippy saw nothing mirthful in her description and her questioning gaze was serious.

"Because you're more fun to be with than a cage full of monkeys. How much ice cream do you want?"

"Two quarts. It's all ordered."

"I'll get it. You can sit here and wonder why I think you're fun to be with."

He loped across the sidewalk and Tippy pushed back her parka with a puzzled expression, then leaned forward in the dim light to pull down a sun shade and study herself in a mirror on its under side. When something in her grave face amused her and brought two dimples into play at the corners of her mouth, she ran down the window and stayed framed in it until she saw Ken come out the door again.

"Listen," she said, when he was near enough to hear, and reaching out for the paper bag of cardboard cartons, "I'm not a moron, am I?"

"I can't answer that one."

He gave her the bag and pressed his gloved thumb against her nose. "But if you are," he said, "the world ought to have about a hundred million more of them. Pull back your feet and I'll crawl over."

Tippy drew herself into a ball, and when Ken was behind the wheel, she said meekly, "I never though about how silly I must sound to other people."

"About as silly as Socrates." The motor purred and they turned around in the empty street. "You do have some crazy ideas," he admitted, wincing when one of his tires scraped the curb. "But on the whole, you're about the biggest *little* guy I ever ran into and you try to carry the world."

"People have to be big," she told him primly, happy with

[184]

her compliment but not daring to admire it until she was alone. "In this queer age we live in, people have to be big and strong."

"Inside, or out?"

"Inside, of course," she answered, smiling, and even taking her turn at teasing. "It's nice to have broad shoulders, like yours, and girls like to go out with them, but it doesn't really matter if one's physically puny. Just a strong heart and a good mind will do the trick," she said with declamatory confidence.

"So you're going to trot your strong heart and your good mind up to Munich and practise on the Germans, is that it? And, there I'll be, in Heidelberg, not knowing how you're coming along."

"Did you take the job?"

"I took it. How did I know you were coming to Munich?" he asked, secretly thinking how fortunate it was that he had decided the matter before he was tempted to stay where a daily telephone call could reach her or a few turns of the wheel would guide his car to her door. And then he weakened with, "I might get down at least once this spring. It isn't so far, and I'll have to know how you're doing."

"But definitely. I may not know myself, but I'll want you to know."

"Would you like to have me around, cherub, darling? Would you?" The words flew out. They escaped his control, and they gave him such a fright that he missed her muffled answer.

"Oh, Ken it's what I want most," she whispered. Then she, too, gasped and clutched her package.

There had been only a foot of seat between them but it became a solid wall. Tippy, on her side, groaned inwardly, "Oh, why did I ever say such a stupid thing! I just spread my feelings right out for him to see." And Ken, condemning himself bitterly for the thoughtless question he had asked, built

[185]

the wall higher by laughing. It was an apologetic laugh, really meant for Colonel and Mrs. Parrish but it brought Tippy's startled gaze over the barrier.

Now, he despises me, she thought. I said silly stupid words and looked like a mooning school girl. I ought to have a lawyer to get up and say, 'I move my clients last sentence be stricken from the record. But she had no lawyer. Her words still stood, and her look that started out with a plea for understanding, not amusement, froze on the way. By the time it reached Ken it was just a long, cold stare that punished him and made him think, She doesn't give a darn about me and I broke a promise by showing how I feel.

So he pretended interest in the ruts. "Darn the things," he muttered, giving the wheel unnecessary wrenches. "Heck, that's a mean one." And all the time his heart was crying, "Even though you don't want to believe what you heard and I don't dare say it again, I meant it. I meant it—darling."

And Tippy turned her eyes on the painted hotel, on cottages along the way, on anything that offered inconsequential comment, while the wall grew higher and higher. Something was lost between them, and they talked haltingly, like two new neighbors getting acquainted over the back fence.

"I—I meant to take Switzy with me," she said, when there was nothing left to see but her own house at the end of the street. "I promised him I would."

The puppy provided a good safe subject, one they could share, and Ken asked guardedly, "Why didn't you?"

"Because he was having his supper. He's—he's such a glutton that I thought I'd have time to put my skis away and get out the car before he finished," she explained elaborately, "and then—then you were here."

"Yeah, here I was." Ken kept his eyes on the road. He felt he should justify his undesirable presence and returned with meaning, "But don't forget, I was invited. Your mother wanted me to come."

"Well, of course, she did. I did, too." Now was the time, Tippy thought. Now was the time to repair her tactless remark, to make him know she valued him only as the friend he wanted to be; and she plunged in, with her chin too high in the air. "We all depend on you, Ken. Too much, I guess."

"Even when I give bad advice, like agreeing with your father that I thought you ought to go home?"

"Even then." She remembered the advice, and blushed. "I guess I am a nuisance," she admitted, and stopped trying.

But Ken climbed over the wall. He knocked the whole thing down by saying, "Don't talk such rot." And he apologized in a lower tone, "I'm sorry I said something that upset you. I didn't mean to, Tip, believe me."

"*You* said something?" Tippy could stare at him in honest amazement now, and she did. "Why, I . . . you. . . . What did you say?" she asked.

"Not a thing, if you didn't notice it. I thought you didn't like it, that's all."

"But what was it? My goodness." She had two things to consider. His puzzling remark and the joyous fact that she hadn't given herself away. He had been too busy worrying over something he, himself, had said to hear her. "Let me see," she thought aloud, delightfully curious. "I asked if you'd taken the job and you said. . . ."

"Skip it, Tip. I said I'd taken it, so let it go at that."

"But after that, you said. . . ." Her eyes were round with amazement and she discovered breathlessly, "You called me 'cherub, darling.' Did you think that made me mad?"

"I didn't know. You clammed up and I felt like a fool."

"Oh, Ken!" Tippy's little face was bright in the light from the dashlight's glow. "People are always calling me darling!" she cried. "Our family passes darlings and honeys around like candy. I didn't even notice it—or I didn't *know* I noticed it, but I must have, because I remember it. And it must have been what made me say. . . ." She clamped her lips together

[187]

as the car swung into the driveway. "Let's forget what either one of us said. Shall we? Hm?" she asked, so tremulous with happiness that she almost missed a forlorn black ball of fur on the portico steps.

Switzy had sat on the step so long that he was chilled clear through his curly fur coat. And his feelings were hurt. It was the first time he had ever been thrust through a door without a definite goal in mind and Tippy to guide him, and it was only by luck and good fortune that he had found his way around the house alone, to this cold spot. And it was dark. It was dark all around the two bright spots of light that blinded him. And since instinct told him his beloved Tippy was behind the spots, he prepared for a dangerous journey down the steps. Coming up had been hard, but going down took courage, and he hoped she would be kind enough to discover his plight and come to aid him.

Tippy watched her puppy's scrambling descent, and longed to run to him; but Ken's answer was more important, and she waited with her hand on the door handle until he made a promise that seemed to have a future, by saying, "We'll put everything completely out of our minds for a long time to come." Then she thrust the ice cream at him and ran.

"Oh, Switzy, Switzy," she crooned, catching up her weeping explorer. "I didn't mean to go off and leave you. It's all right, now." The puppy made sniffing, snuffling noises against her ear, and she said reproachfully to Ken as he came up, "Why did you let me *do* it?"

"Now, how do you like that!" he returned gruffly, putting them back on the friendly basis where they belonged. "She blames *me* for it, Switz, when I didn't even know whether you were still alive, or not."

"Of course, he's alive. Feel that, and see." Tippy's face had taken a thorough washing and she let Ken have the kisses still flowing from Switzy's inexhaustible source. Then she took his hand and swung it companionably as they went up the steps.

"*Grüss Gott,* Jochen," she said, when the door flew magically open. "We brought the ice cream." She watched Ken hand over the paper bag with a package of cigarettes on top, and dropping her canvas coat on a chair, sighed reluctantly, "I'll have to go dress, but I won't be a minute. Do you mind hunting up Mums or Dad? They should be around."

"I'll find them. No rush."

"Yes, there is." She set Switzy on the first step of the stairs and went up one above him. "Come on, little boy," she coaxed, bending down to give him a boost that sent him up the step on his nose. "Oh, you're too slow," she laughed, picking him up, which was just what he wanted.

Colonel Parrish had come to the living room door and Ken went off with him. The cold air had electrified his two little sprouts of hair so that they waved informally, and Tippy gave a glad chuckle while she watched them.

"Really," she told Switzy, "not many girls have as much to be happy about as I have. They don't have you, for one thing." She ran up the rest of the way and carried him through the hall to her room. "Now sit still," she commanded, settling him on the bed where he had a good view of the room but no chance to hang on the end of everything she took from the closet.

Now and then she gave him a piece of crumpled paper to play with or an empty match box, and when she had slipped on a long, brown taffeta dress, she gathered up the folds of her full skirt, and said, "Be patient," and sat quickly down at her desk. Her letter lay in the drawer where she had left it and it seemed important to end it now, quickly, while everything was straight in her mind; so, after a hurried glance at the last page, she found her pen and dashed off :

"*P.S. Peter. I won't need the cable now, because I've told them. But writing to you helped me a lot. I wanted to come home, even more than I've made you know in the letter. I'll try to come next year, for college. But if I can't, I'll be there all the following year, when you're a first classman. And if I seem mvddled again and too old and far away, don't let me. Please, Peter, don't let me.*

                                                    Tippy"

It was an almost illegible scrawl, but she gathered up the sheets and returned them to their hiding place in her desk. Then she scooped up Switzy, and with her skirt rustling behind her on the stairs ran lightly down to her party.